Dominated

Jaid Black

The Possession

Kris Torrence wants to experience sexual submission to a man once in her lifetime. Having a reputation for being a sedate, boring professor, nobody at her university job suspects anything when she signs up to work for five days at an exclusive gentlemen's resort that caters to wealthy men seeking submissive sex slaves...

Jack McKenna has been Dr. Kris Torrence's longtime nemesis. When he sees a naked sex slave walking around the resort whose long, dark red hair reminds him of the woman who will have nothing to do with him, he decides to buy her. When he sees her face for the first time, Jack and Kris will both get the shock of a lifetime...

The Addiction

John Calder has everything most men would kill for — golden-Adonis looks, endless money, a steely reputation as a savvy businessman and beautiful women throwing themselves at his feet. Then he meets Shelli Rodgers, a quirky, klutzy Ph.D. student who takes John on an emotional and sensual journey, giving him the one thing he's never attained — happiness.

An Ellora's Cave Publication

www.ellorascave.com

Dominated

ISBN 9781419969263
ALL RIGHTS RESERVED.
The Possession Copyright © 2002 Jaid Black
The Addiction Copyright © 2011 Jaid Black
The Addiction edited by Kelli Collins.
Cover design and photography by Syneca.
Model: Axl & Lisa.

Trade paperback publication 2013

With the exception of quotes used in reviews, this book may not be reproduced or used in whole or in part by any means existing without written permission from the publisher, Ellora's Cave Publishing, Inc.® 1056 Home Avenue, Akron OH 44310-3502.

Warning: The unauthorized reproduction or distribution of this copyrighted work is illegal. Criminal copyright infringement, including infringement without monetary gain, is investigated by the FBI and is punishable by up to 5 years in federal prison and a fine of $250,000. (http://www.fbi.gov/ipr/)

This book is a work of fiction and any resemblance to persons, living or dead, or places, events or locales is purely coincidental. The characters are productions of the author's imagination and used fictitiously.

The publisher and author(s) acknowledge the trademark status and trademark ownership of all trademarks, service marks and word marks mentioned in this book.

The publisher does not have any control over and does not assume any responsibility for author or third-party Web sites or their content.

DOMINATED
Jaid Black

ಸಿ

THE POSSESSION
~9~

THE ADDICTION
~147~

THE POSSESSION
ରୁ

Prologue

ა

Kris Torrence took a deep, contemplative breath as she stared at herself in the mirror of her postage stamp sized bathroom. *This can't be as good as it gets,* she thought morosely. *I can't be as good as I get...*

She was pretty enough, she supposed, with her wine-red hair and cat-like green eyes. Undoubtedly more average than beautiful but pretty enough that she should have been dating, should have been leading a more exciting life. Yet she wasn't and didn't.

Thirty-four and never married, Kris was content with being single—enjoyed it even. She liked living alone, relished the freedom of being able to do what she wanted when she wanted to do it without having to confer with a man about her plans for the evening. Being single definitely has its rewards.

But, she conceded, it has its drawbacks too.

Loneliness was the biggest of them. Lots and lots of lonely nights spent staring at the empty pillow next to hers in the queen-sized bed, fantasizing about falling in love, fantasizing about risqué sexual situations she'd realistically never find herself in. She was a normal woman after all. *She had needs.*

But mostly, she sighed, mostly she just fantasized about companionship.

However, she reminded herself, her chin going up a notch, she wasn't lonely for companionship altogether, just lonely for male companionship. And, she thought pointedly as her cat Hercules sauntered from the bathroom and toward the kitchen with a *meeow*, human male companionship in particular.

She winced, wondering not for the first time if she had inadvertently turned into the living portrait of an old maid without even realizing it. Hercules, she thought grimly, was but one of a grand total of five felines living in her apartment.

Five cats! Kris grimaced. When in the hell had she managed to acquire five cats? It's as if she'd fallen asleep one night a young woman and woke up the next morning a pathetic spinster.

She rolled her eyes at herself in the mirror. "Stop it, Kris," she chastised her image. "You're not a spinster and you know it. You're just..." She sighed. "You're just lonely and bored."

It was the truth and she knew it. Yes, she was thirty-four. Yes, she had never been married. No, she wasn't dating anyone and hadn't in at least six months.

But overall she loved her life. She enjoyed her tenured position as a professor of anthropology at San Francisco State University, found the research she did on other cultures with her graduate students invigorating and challenging.

And, she sniffed, there was nothing wrong with owning cats. Many cats. Lots of cats. All kinds of cats. Smallish short-haired ones, tall and lanky long-haired ones, big fat furball ones, and —

Her teeth gritted. Okay, so maybe she owned too many goddamned cats.

But other than the fact she was a one-woman humane society, there wasn't anything wrong with her life and she knew it. And really, she thought with a grin as Zeus jumped up on the bathroom sink and purred against her hand while his rough tongue lapped at her skin there, there wasn't anything wrong with being a hopeless, dyed-in-the-wool, lover of felines. It's just that...

Her grin slowly faded as she stared at herself in the mirror. It's just that she was a bit tired of the status quo, a bit tired of leading a boring, complacent existence.

And, she acknowledged as she drew in a deep breath, she had needs like any other normal woman. She was at her sexual peak for goodness sake—hardly the time in her life to remain celibate due to complacency!

She wanted to once—*just once*—do something wild and crazy, something completely out of character from the Dr. Kris Torrence everyone at the university knew and respected. Something brazen and reckless enough to give her a lifetime of memories she could hug close to her heart whenever she was in the mood to wax sentimental on rebellious days gone by. She was getting older and...

She sighed. In her youth, and onward into her twenties, she had always done the right thing, the proper thing. As a teenager she had done what the nuns at the parochial school she'd attended had expected of her, she had been the good girl her parents had wanted her to be, and...

And she was sick as she didn't know what of being that good girl. No thirty-four year-old woman needs to conform to the expectations of others when those expectations were not her own. Or, more to the point, no thirty-four year-old woman *should* conform to the expectations of others when those expectations were not her own.

Kris nibbled at her lower lip as her eyes slowly strayed down to the bathroom sink counter and toward the magazine lying open on it. She mentally resisted rereading the classified ad she'd been compelled to study for what felt like a thousand times in the past three days. But in the end she found her hands reaching for it and her heart rate picking up as her eyes soaked in the words:

Hotel Atlantis is currently searching for select females to work in our exclusive gentlemen's resort situated on a private island off the coast of San Francisco. Pay is exceptional for exceptional females as our resort accommodates only the wealthiest of clientele. Women comfortable in the role of submissive are especially needed. Island excursions last anywhere from 3-7 days...

Kris blew out a breath as she reread the part of the ad that most appealed to her.

Women comfortable in the role of submissive are especially needed.

It had always been a fantasy, she conceded as she chewed on her bottom lip. A very big, got-her-wet-every-time-she-thought-about-it fantasy...

To be submissive to a man. To play slave to his master. To allow a man to tie her up and do anything he wanted to her—

It was something no good girl would do.

It was something she wanted to do very badly.

Her heartbeat sped up. *Just for one night*, she promised herself. *Or in this case, just for one island excursion.*

It wasn't as if nobody had ever heard of Hotel Atlantis. On the contrary, everybody who lived in or around the Bay area knew precisely what the resort was and whom the resort catered to, even if it wasn't the sort of topic one tended to bring up in casual conversation.

Hotel Atlantis was *the* exclusive place that elite businessmen went for sun, fun, and no-strings-attached sex with any paid woman, and as many paid women, of their choosing.

If you want to live out your deepest sexual fantasies without anybody of your acquaintance finding out about it, this would be the place to do it, Kris. She took another deep breath. *There is no way in hell that any of your male colleagues at the university make enough money to frequent that island!*

Kris set the magazine down on the bathroom sink counter and resumed staring at herself in the mirror. She doubted such an exclusive gentlemen's retreat as Hotel Atlantis would want to hire a woman as average looking as she was anyway. But maybe if she let her long and curly wine-red hair down from the bun, and applied a little bit of makeup, and...

Her lips pinched together in a frown. Perhaps if she underwent a complete reconstructive overhaul of her average face she could talk Hotel Atlantis into letting her work one excursion.

She bristled at that. As if she wanted to work in a place where she was destined to be the ugliest woman on the entire island! Especially, she thought morosely, when the entire reason she wanted to go in the first place wasn't for the money as the other women no doubt were, but to get a little action.

She sighed as she glanced back down at the ad.

Hotel Atlantis will be conducting in-person interviews throughout the entire last week of March in the San Francisco area. Call John Calder today at 555-3212 to—

She stopped reading, her finger tracing the outline of the printed telephone number. "On the other hand," she murmured, "it can't hurt to at least call the guy."

Closing her eyes briefly and taking a steadying breath, she shut the magazine and slowly turned around to face the exit to the bathroom.

Nervous and feeling surprisingly giddy, Kris swallowed hard in her throat as she found herself walking toward the kitchen—and the telephone. When she reached it, when the cordless phone's receiver was firmly in hand, she took a deep breath before pounding out the telephone number she'd committed to memory three days ago.

"This is insane," she muttered to herself as she waited for someone on the other end of the line to pick up. "I must have lost my—"

"Thank you for calling Hotel Atlantis. This is Sheri Carucci. How may I assist you this evening?"

Kris' green eyes widened at the disembodied sound of the throaty voice. Her heartbeat picked up so dramatically that she idly wondered for one hysterical moment if it would come thumping out of her chest.

"Hello? This is Hotel Atlantis. Hello?"

Her breathing grew labored as her heartbeat climbed impossibly higher.

"Very funny, buddy. Listen," the throaty-turned-annoyed voice asked, "you wanna book a stay on the island or not?"

Terrified and feeling way out of her element, Kris' hand flew to the wall console, preparing to hang up. But just as she was about to end the connection, just as her fingers were about to press the disconnect button, her gaze was snagged by a photograph hanging on the wall a foot away.

Her eyes narrowed into slits. The photograph was of herself and her five cats.

If only I had been wearing a parochial schoolgirl uniform in that picture the pathetic good girl imagery would be complete!

Kris' nostrils flared as she planted her hand firmly on her hip so it couldn't fly up to the disconnect button of its own accord and nervously end the connection with Madame Throaty Voice against her volition.

"My name is Kris," she determinedly gritted out into the receiver, her chin thrusting up. And with the conviction and resolution of a recovering alcoholic at a group prevention meeting, she added loudly and cathartically, her nostrils flaring impossibly further, "and I'm a submissive!"

"Hold on a sec," Madame Throaty Voice replied with a yawn. "Let me transfer you upstairs to that department."

Kris grunted.

Chapter One
Three weeks later

ഌ

"Good morning, Dr. Torrence."

"Good morning, Dr. Moore."

Kris smiled fully as she strolled into the faculty lounge, her good mood evident. She was dressed in a conservative navy business skirt that ended at the knee, a white cotton shirt that was buttoned all the way to the top, and her mass of dark red curls was secured in a tight bun at the nape of her neck. Completing her usual ensemble was a pair of black spectacles perched at the tip of her nose.

Clearly, she felt better than she looked. But then she'd never placed much importance on fashion anyway.

Kris inclined her head to Dr. Moore as she strutted by him, feeling as though she was on cloud nine. She just prayed nobody in the anthropology department figured out why she was in such good spirits. She could hardly believe it herself.

"How are you doing today?" she asked conversationally. "I'm sorry I'm late." *I was busy packing my bags for my trip to Hotel Atlantis!* "Has anything happened around here I should know about?"

Dr. Moore nodded, his pompous tone as annoying as it had ever been. "Quite a bit actually..."

She listened to her colleague's rather long-winded answer with half an ear as she poured herself a cup of what most people would call beans and water, but what the university called, or tried to pass off as at any rate, coffee.

Kris ignored Dr. Moore as she sipped from the steamy mug of cheap quasi-Columbian brew, and reflected back on the conversation she'd had with Sheri Carucci last week.

"*After meeting with you, John felt that you were perfect for the position, doll. He'd like to have you work the five-day island excursion slated to start one week from today. Or is that too soon?*"

"N-No," Kris had stammered out, her heart thumping madly against her chest. She hadn't used up a single day of vacation time this year so she knew she had the days coming to her. "He...he actually thought I'd fit in there?" she asked hesitantly, uncertain as to whether or not she'd heard her correctly. Or that Madame Throaty Voice had heard John Calder correctly.

Sheri chuckled, a grin in her voice. "You sound surprised."

"I am surprised," she said in a bewildered monotone, her jaw slack.

"*Well don't be,*" Sheri replied. "*Besides, these rich guys really go for the innocent, good-girl look.*"

Her bemusement vanished as her teeth gritted. "I am not," Kris said distinctly, each word precise, "innocent. Nor am I a good girl." She slashed her hand through the air for emphasis, though Sheri couldn't see that.

"*Uh huh.*"

Kris sighed. "Okay maybe I look that way." She sighed again. "Okay maybe I am that way. But please believe me when I say I don't want to be that way."

"*Hmm,*" Sheri said noncommittally, her tone amused. "*Why do I get the feeling you don't want this job for the money, doll?*"

When Kris said nothing, merely sat quietly on the other end of the connection worrying her lip as she wondered if she'd inadvertently given her ulterior motives away, Sheri chuckled again.

"*It's okay. Your secret is safe with me. Hey! If rich men can come here to get their rocks off then why can't we women?*"

Kris found herself smiling into the receiver. And immediately taking a liking to one Madame Throaty Voice. "Why indeed," she murmured.

And so the chartered flight to Atlantis Island had been booked. For tonight.

She gulped.

"Oh," Dr. Moore continued, breaking her out of her reverie, "I almost forgot to mention that Mr. McKenna is in your office." He shook his head, perturbed. "He's waiting to speak to you," he said disdainfully as he adjusted his tie.

Kris frowned at Dr. Moore. "Mr. McKenna? As in Jack McKenna?" She sighed as she looked at her colleague, for once sharing in Dr. Moore's less than hospitable mood. He was the last person she wanted to see today, especially considering how frazzled her nerves already were from the impending journey to Hotel Atlantis tonight. "Oh no, not him again."

"Afraid so."

"What does he want this time?" she asked resignedly, realizing as she did that if Jack McKenna wanted to speak to her she had little choice but to acquiesce. As the owner of the multimillion-dollar construction company that had built half the high-rises in downtown San Francisco, and as a corporate financier of the university's anthropology department in particular, Jack McKenna was allowed to get away with more than most. A fact that irritated Kris enough to make her teeth grind together from merely looking at the big bruiser.

"Why don't you ask him yourself," a dark voice growled from behind her.

Kris whipped around, almost spilling her coffee at her surprise as she did so. She hesitantly glanced toward Dr. Moore who was uncomfortably clearing his throat while pretending to readjust his tie.

Her chin went up determinedly as she returned her gaze to Jack McKenna. She met the calculating dark eyes of her nemesis dead-on, refusing to be intimidated by him and his bullying ways. Her eyes narrowed as she considered him, sizing him up as one would an opponent in the boxing ring.

One dark eyebrow rose bemusedly, a never-before-seen grin tugging at one corner of his mouth.

Kris grunted. Jack McKenna was handsome enough, she supposed. For a big bruiser type anyway. He was a tall man—probably stood around six foot four—and at forty-two years of age was still as thick with muscle as any pro-football linebacker. His hair was short and dark and given to the slightest hint of curl, his big body bronzed with tan.

She knew that he had worked his way up through the ranks of the construction company he now owned, having started at the bottom as a laborer. She could surmise from the heavy musculature of his body that he probably hadn't given up his former trade altogether when he'd bought out his uncle and taken over McKenna Construction, for he had the strong and powerful look of a man who was accustomed to heavy laboring.

Not that she'd noticed or anything, she sniffed.

"You wanted to see me, Mr. McKenna?"

With Dr. Salazar on vacation until tomorrow that left Kris in the apparently pitiful position of being the most tenured, which meant she'd be the one obliged to hear Jack McKenna growl out his latest demands. Again.

Six months ago when Dr. Salazar had been on a dig in Mexico, Jack McKenna had prowled around the department with his demands. Three months before that when Dr. Salazar had been at a conference in Hawaii, he had come around growling again. If she didn't know better, she'd start to wonder if the damn man waited for her boss to disappear just so he could growl at her in particular. But that was ludicrous to think, of course.

That black eyebrow rose again as he regarded her, a habit of his that always left her feeling decidedly irritated. It was as if he was sizing her up—and finding her lacking. But then a man like Jack McKenna, a wealthy man who'd dated just about every brainless bimbo in the Bay area, would look down his nose at a woman so average in appearance as herself. Physically she was his inferior and she knew it.

His dark gaze methodically roamed over her body, starting at her legs, working slowly up to her breasts and lingering, then climbing higher to her face. She felt a bit flustered when her nipples hardened at the tingling of sensual awareness that passed through her, but ignored the feeling and quickly pushed it aside.

Besides, she reminded herself as she raised one of her wine-red eyebrows and met his determined stare with a challenging one of her own, Jack McKenna was probably just trying to intimidate her. As always. Once a bully, always a bully.

It was ironic indeed that the very sort of man Kris wanted to experience submission with in bed was standing before her, yet she knew she'd never hand herself over to a man like this one in a trillion years. Not that the multimillionaire construction worker cum CEO had ever expressed any interest in doing so anyway, she thought grimly.

But if he had tried to take her to bed, she knew she would have said no. Not only because a messy affair could cause problems for her at the university, but also because Jack McKenna wasn't the sort of man who would take dominance and submission as a mere sexual game. He was the type of arrogant male who would take it literally, expecting a woman to cater to him always, whether in the bedroom or out of it.

Definitely not her type.

Even if he was masculine sexuality personified.

"Hell yes I want to see you," he growled. He jabbed a finger in the general direction of her office door. "Let's go talk, lady."

Or masculine idiocy personified, she thought with down-turned lips.

Kris frowned severely, even as she decided that she might as well get the royal summons over and done with. The faster she listened to his growling session, the faster the big bruiser would be gone. But, she decided, she would not speak privately with him until she set him straight on one score.

"My name is *Doctor* Torrence," she said pointedly, sounding as pompous as Dr. Moore at that moment. "And if that is too long and too complicated of a name for your brain to absorb, then *Doctor* will suffice." She inclined her head. "I did not, sir, spend eight years in college earning my Ph.D. to be talked down to as though I am an idiotic twit."

He sighed, then pinched the bridge of his nose as he seemingly gathered himself together. No doubt a delaying tactic to keep himself from snapping at her.

He glanced up, his jaw clenched, his dark eyes blazing into her green ones. "Look lady…"

She clucked her tongue, fascinated by the vein throbbing at his temple.

"*Doctor* Torrence…" he growled.

She smiled, then nodded. "You wanted to speak with me in private?" she asked sweetly. Too sweetly.

His nostrils flared as he narrowed his dark gaze at her. "Yes," he hissed.

A hiss. She'd never heard him hiss before and found herself wondering what precisely it meant. Odd as it was, she was good at detecting Jack McKenna's moods. Not that it took a Ph.D. in anthropology to do so for he only seemed to have two moods in total: surly and surlier.

Telling herself it didn't matter, and that she had better things to do with her time than quarrel with an overgrown Neanderthal—such as prepare for her chartered flight tonight!—she waved a hand easterly and strolled toward her office door.

Her nemesis was quiet for the entire walk down the hallway, which Kris found distressingly odd for such a huge and generally loud man. She felt a queer premonition pass over her, that sort of bizarre jolt that makes the hair at the nape of one's neck stir when you somehow become aware of the fact that you are being watched.

She stiffened. Jack McKenna doesn't watch like a normal man does.

Jack McKenna studies. He calculates. He assesses.

He hunts.

She swallowed a bit roughly, wondering what it was precisely that he was hunting today. Kris didn't fool herself for even a moment into thinking the big bruiser had all of a sudden become taken with her as a woman. On every occasion she'd been obliged to deal with him, and admittedly she'd seen to it that those occasions were few and far between, he had shown her nothing but hostility, disdain, and even, for whatever reason, resentment.

Perhaps he resented the fact that she was a woman with a Ph.D. Perhaps he resented the fact that she had red hair. Perhaps he resented the fact that her automobile of choice was a conservative, no-frills Volvo. Perhaps he resented the fact that—

Bah! Who knew what his reasons were.

Where Jack McKenna was concerned, one could never be certain of anything. So basically you were best off not even trying to figure them out to begin with.

Kris closed the door behind him after he entered her small, modest office. Motioning for him to have a seat, she decided to ignore him when he merely grunted without sitting down. Sighing, she seated herself behind her desk and smiled as politely as she could. She folded her hands on the desk before her and met his gaze. "How can I help you, Mr. McKenna?"

He frowned as he stared at her in silence, his dark expression brooding. They faced off in stark quiet for what felt like the tensest hour of Kris' life, their gazes locked in mutual challenge, when in fact it couldn't have been more than thirty seconds that had already ticked by.

She grew increasingly anxious on the inside, her heart rate picking up dramatically, but on the outside she looked ice-cool. And then finally, thankfully, he opened his mouth to speak. But whatever it might have been that he had been about to say was interrupted when Dr. Salazar made an unexpected appearance into the office.

Kris blew out a breath as she stood up, relieved. She wouldn't be obliged to deal with the growling grump after all.

"Alma," Jack said politely if a bit gruffly. Almost as though he was disappointed by the fact that their impending conversation had been interrupted. But then that made no sense really.

Jack respectfully inclined his head when he stood up to greet the department head, inducing Kris' forehead to wrinkle. This was the first time she had ever seen Jack McKenna and Alma Salazar interact and she had to wonder at it. Kris had always assumed that the bruiser probably treated the older woman as surly as he did the rest of the world. Apparently that assumption had been wrong.

She frowned when she wondered if Jack saved up all of his bad manners for her alone.

Jerk.

"It's good to see you, Jack," Dr. Salazar said sincerely, causing Kris to blink. But then Kris couldn't imagine anybody being happy to see Jack McKenna. It was like the Whos down in Who-ville being happy to see the Grinch before he'd reformed his wicked ways. "I came back from vacation a day early because I'm behind with paperwork. I'm glad I didn't miss you. But I see that Krissy here was helping you."

She winced at Dr. Salazar's casual usage of the name Krissy. She winced again when she realized the feminine sounding name hadn't gone unnoticed by the Grinch. That damn eyebrow of his shot up again as he flicked his gaze toward her.

"Yes," he said dryly, his voice a low growl. "Krissy and I were just getting ready to discuss the problems down at your team's excavation site."

Kris frowned, her hands folding under her breasts.

Dr. Salazar's eyebrows drew together quizzically. "Problems, Jack? I'm afraid I don't follow."

He nodded. "Yeah. Problems. The problem being it isn't excavated yet. Look," he said in the calmest tone of voice Kris had ever heard him use, "I don't mind delaying my men by a day or two so your team can finish digging up those old bones we happened across, but time is money, Alma, and your team is taking up a hell of a lot of my time."

Dr. Salazar nodded. "I understand, Jack. Krissy and I will get right on it ourselves." She patted him on the shoulder, an affectionate and platonic gesture. "No need to worry. We'll finish excavating it tonight."

Tonight?

Kris' eyes widened. *Of all nights, please not tonight!* she mentally wailed.

Jack McKenna turned his head and stared at Kris as though he was working her out in his mind—as though he had figured out he was thwarting her from doing something she had really wanted to do tonight. And damned if he didn't look pleased by that realization.

Jerk!

"Good," he murmured, his gaze never leaving Kris.

She stiffened, her chin notching up, as it was apt to do whenever she felt defensive. "I'll be more than happy to excavate the site with you, Dr. Salazar," she said in a professionally clipped tone as she tore her gaze away from Jack's. "But if you want me to be a part of the excavation I'm afraid it will have to wait until I return from my vacation in a week." She nodded definitively, letting it be known that in this one particular instance she would not waver. She had a solid reputation for being a team player, so she wasn't worried Alma would think poorly of her.

Dr. Salazar inclined her head, affirming her assumption.

Jack frowned, his dark eyes broodingly raking over Kris. "Why?" he barked. "You going somewhere with a guy or something?"

"Or something," she said sweetly, letting him wonder. She decided to ignore the fact that his interest in the subject did weird things to her belly. Like put butterflies inside of it.

Nerves. It had to be nerves that had made her stomach flutter. The only thing Jack McKenna did to her belly was give it indigestion.

Kris picked up her purse, nodding at Jack and Alma as she strolled toward the door. "I'll leave you two to talk. I have a lot of work to do in the lab today before I leave for vacation."

She blew out a breath. And a lot of mental preparation to perform in anticipation of tonight's flight to the exclusive, private island.

Chapter Two

ഔ

Kris closed her eyes, took a deep, steadying breath in a futile effort to calm her frayed nerves, and then resumed staring out of the six-seater airplane's small peephole of a window.

She wondered what John Calder would think when he saw her, for she hadn't had time to change out of her drab business clothing in between leaving the university and catching the chartered flight to the island. But then again, John had warned her that she wouldn't need clothes at Hotel Atlantis because she'd be totally naked for the entire five days...

She nibbled on her lower lip, her green eyes wide.

What the hell had she been thinking, signing up to become a submissive sex slave for five days?

She sighed, absently rubbing her temples as the lush and surprisingly tropical looking Atlantis Island slowly came into view. It's just that she really wanted to try this, she reminded herself. Just once.

Besides, Kris considered herself to be a very good judge of character. John Calder might be a smart businessman who had figured out a way to make enviable money for himself and the women who worked on the island, but she had a good feeling about him as a person and believed wholeheartedly that the assurances he'd given to her were nothing short of the truth.

He and his sister Sheri would take good care of her. They never allowed men on the island who hadn't gone through and passed intense personal screenings and background checks.

Indeed, Sheri has assured her that most of the patrons of the island were regular clients that she and John had known for at least five years or more. And all of them were the types of high profile men who would rather be on their best behavior for the women who worked in Hotel Atlantis than do something stupid and chance that a potentially damaging situation might be aired in public as dirty laundry for all the world to see.

In other words, Kris had nothing to worry about. The male patrons were horny and rascally, but nobody would dare harm her.

She blew out a breath.

As the island loomed in closer, her heart rate picked up dramatically. This was as exciting as it was terrifying, she mentally conceded.

Taking a brief glance around the tiny cabin at the other four female passengers on the chartered plane, she idly wondered to herself if they were as nervous as she was. She doubted it. All four of them had the calm, collected look of professionals. And all four of them were perfect in appearance with their gorgeously painted faces, firm bodies, and golden blonde good looks.

She sighed. They were so beautiful—too beautiful. She'd probably have to pay one of the paying customers to get herself a little action, she thought with a frown.

Ah well. It was either this or five days with the cats.

Kris straightened in her seat and decided to focus on the upcoming night that lay ahead of her rather than on things destined to make her a nervous wreck. Tonight was no more than an orientation of sorts, she reminded herself. So it really wasn't necessary to get all flustered. The male patrons wouldn't begin arriving until some time tomorrow afternoon.

Then and only then would she work herself into a knot of raw, frayed, and otherwise exposed nerves.

*****

Leaning against his expensive oak desk, a glass of bourbon in hand, John Calder grinned at Kris' nervousness. "If you can't get naked in front of me without blushing, my dear, then how are you going to deal with it tomorrow when a group of rich, horny men are all vying for your attention, anxious to fuck you?" He held the short glass up, preparing to sip from it as he studied her. "I don't mean to be crude, but I don't want misunderstandings either. You do realize that's what you're here for, don't you?"

Kris sighed as she let her hair down, the tight bun spilling a cascade of dark red ringlets down to her lower back. Her hair, like Samson, had always been her strength, her best feature. She suspected even her new employer agreed when the sight of her curls cascading down made him stiffen in a noticeable region. She averted her gaze, quickly glancing away.

"My dear Kris," he murmured from across the room. "You could make even a man like me forget how jaded he's become."

Her head shot up. Her forehead wrinkled. "Huh?"

"Never mind," he said with a sigh that sounded almost tragic, and left her feeling decidedly confused. He set down the glass of bourbon and walked slowly toward her. "I don't want you doing this if it's not something you want to do. If it's money you need, there are plenty of ways—"

"It's not the money," she quickly blurted out. She took a deep breath. Dear lord, she didn't want him to send her away. Not when she'd made it this far! "Listen, Mr. Calder..."

"John," he corrected with a smile.

She nodded. "How apropos." She grinned when he chuckled at that, her nervousness fading with every moment she spent in his presence. "It's not the money," she admitted again, her expression growing serious. "It's just something I need to do. For me." She sighed as she glanced away, kicking off her no-nonsense pumps at the same time. "I own five cats," she said morosely. "And I'm a member of Mensa."

John hid a smile. "I see." He was quiet as he watched her slowly disrobe, saying nothing until she stood before him wearing only her bra and panties.

Kris took a deep breath as she glanced up at him, her shoulders straight and stiff.

He chuckled. "Try not to look as though you're facing your executioner and you might enjoy these five days a bit more."

She grinned at him, and then laughed. "You're very good at talking a woman out of her clothing, you know." She shook her head. "If you were anyone else I probably would have bolted in fright the moment the plane landed."

"We all have our talents," he teased.

Kris cocked her head as she studied his face. He was a very handsome man, she had to admit. Tall, muscular, golden brown hair, and darkly tanned. And his playful personality was nothing at all like that damn Jack McKenna's grizzly one.

Now why are you thinking about Jack McKenna, idiot? she chastised herself. *He's safely ensconced in San Francisco and you're on Atlantis Island, standing in the owner's office in Hotel Atlantis, about to make your deepest fantasies a reality tomorrow.*

She chalked up her inner musings to nerves again. Perhaps it was easier to her state of mind to think about dealing with the big bruiser because he was a known, if irritating, entity. But this situation, and this man, was definitely novel.

Kris blushed as she reached behind her back and began unfastening her bra. "I guess I better get over my embarrassment. And quickly."

"And burn those horrid old maid clothes while you're at it," he said a bit thickly.

Her eyes flew to his groin, and she immediately noticed that his bulge there had grown. Only instead of reacting shyly to his erection this time, she found herself feeling more powerful. Well, still a little shy. But undeniably giddy.

John Calder had access to any beautiful woman of his choosing, after all. But his penis was getting turned on by ordinary her.

She finished unfastening her bra and allowed it to drop to the floor. Her shoulders relaxed a bit when she saw that his blue eyes had narrowed in arousal.

"You have nice breasts," he said softly. "Full, natural, lightly tanned like the rest of you…and your nipples are exquisite."

She blushed, despite her resolve not to again.

"And now the panties," he said firmly.

Kris took a steadying breath, then blew it out as she removed her boring cotton panties. He was right about her clothing, she conceded. She did dress like an old maid.

When she at last stood before him completely naked, her breasts and mons bared to him, she watched him look his fill at her, his eyes raking over her nude form.

"Very nice," he murmured, walking the scant foot toward her that separated them. "I have a friend who loves redheads, you know. Obsesses over them actually." He grinned. "He'll be here tonight. I have a feeling that when he sees you tomorrow, all bets are off for the other patrons. You'll be his for the entire time. He won't share this exquisite beauty with anyone else."

She shook her head as she smiled at him. He was making her feel sexy, bolstering her self-confidence, and she appreciated it more than words could say. Lord knows that tomorrow she'd need all the self-confidence she could get. "Thanks for saying that," she said quietly. "Even if you don't mean it."

Her breath caught in surprise when his warm palm covered her left breast, then left in a rush when his thumb began plumping up the nipple.

"You're a very sexy woman," he said thickly. "And if it wasn't for the fact that I have a business to run these next five days, I'd order you to my own bed."

His usage of the word *order* immediately caused her clit to swell—the usual reaction she had when reading about female submission in books. Funny that it had taken a commanding word from the handsome man to get her wet, though. Because when a man as commanding of nature as Jack McKenna growled at her...

Bah! Her nemesis was the last man she wanted to think about just now. Even if the Grinch's growling did secretly make her wet every time he snapped at her. It's just that his surly attitude and gruff nature embodied the very ideal she held up for what a master should be like. Or for the kind of master she wanted to be a slave to for five days.

But Jack McKenna wasn't the type to view master and slave as a game, she reminded herself. *Not that he wants you anyway, idiot!*

"Jump up on the table and spread your legs for me," John said in a non-threatening tone, bringing Kris back from her thoughts.

Her green eyes widened at the command, but she did as he'd asked her to and hopped up on the table behind her. That done, and growing increasingly aroused, she spread her thighs wide open and, her heart thumping madly, watched as he stared at her exposed vagina.

"Very nice pussy," he drawled softly as he drew closer, his gaze fastened on it. "Now put your hands behind you on the table so your gorgeous tits are thrust up even higher."

She blew out a nervous breath and complied.

His eyes raked over her naked breasts as his hand reached toward her mons. "Very nice," he murmured. His right hand began to gently stroke her, his thumb zeroing in on the clit. She gasped, her nipples instantly stabbing up into the cool air of the office.

The Possession

"That's right," he said in low tones as he expertly massaged her. He smiled when she bucked up her hips on a soft moan and ground her swollen pussy up against his palm. "Let yourself go, sweetheart. Drench my hand."

Her head fell back on a groan as she came hard and quickly for her new and very temporary employer. She hadn't been touched like this by a man in over a year, let alone mounted by one as she would be during the excursion.

Even as heat rushed to her face and her nipples jutted out from the impact of the orgasm, she realized, of course, that John's only intention was to condition her to a stranger's touch. She knew it was nothing personal and that when he was finished with her the next woman would be led in for the same conditioning.

This was to prepare her for the next five days, when lots of strange men would be touching her. Which was what she wanted.

Wasn't it?

Or maybe, perhaps, she wanted only one man doing these things to her.

But it was too late to turn back now, she decided. And she really did want to have one wild experience to look fondly back upon.

Her breathing labored, her heart rate wild, she watched as John dipped a finger into her wet flesh, pulled it out, and sensually sucked it dry. He smiled. "Very nice."

She half laughed and half snorted as she sat up straight and closed her thighs. "I bet you say that to all the girls."

He didn't bother to deny it, which for some reason she found amusing.

"No worries," he promised her with a wink. "You'll do just fine tomorrow."

Chapter Three

Jack McKenna stalked up the front steps to Hotel Atlantis feeling even surlier than usual, which was saying a lot. Dr. Salazar's excavation of the construction site had gone on longer than he had expected, the flight to the island had been bumpy, and truth be told, he wasn't in much of a mood to be here anyway.

He had come because his best friend had asked him to join him for a week of pleasure. John tended to worry over him like an older brother, when in fact John was two years younger than his own forty-two.

Maybe his best buddy was right, Jack decided with a scowl. Maybe the best way to get that damn little prissy witch out of his mind was to work her out of it.

Preferably with some deep, violent thrusting into a warm, awaiting woman. Better yet because of the dangerous way he felt just now, a warm, awaiting, *submissive* woman was what he needed. All the things the prickly Ph.D. was not.

He frowned as he absently pushed open the heavy thatched hut doors that had cost John a pretty penny and were made to resemble the impenetrable wall that separated the natives on Skull Island from their god King Kong.

His eyebrows rose as he stepped inside. On the other side of the doors lay paradise.

The voluptuous naked women wouldn't be prancing around the resort that had been fashioned to bring to mind a jungle oasis until tomorrow, but already young, muscular men were situating thatched tables and imported jungle trees all over, preparing for the onslaught of the wealthy guests who would begin arriving in a few hours time.

Jack grunted. How ironic that men worked their asses off to be as rich as they could be so they wouldn't have to live like primitives, then they turn around and pay his best buddy tens of thousands of dollars a pop to spend a few days living like that very thing.

Only in style, of course. And with lots of naked, willing women, he thought with a half-smile.

He wondered what the prissy little witch would think of his being here.

She'd thumb her nose at the resort, and at him, he thought with a frown. Her type always did.

His smile faded. He couldn't even figure out what it was that had attracted him to the red-haired know-it-all to begin with. She spoke in big sentences, used pompous words, and thought that men like him who didn't have a formal education were beneath her. Worse yet her clothes were plain and drab, her hair was always wrapped into a bun so tight he sometimes found himself wondering if her cat-like eyes would bug out of her head, and nine days out of ten she had on the ugliest, thickest black spectacles he'd ever had the displeasure of seeing.

Goddamn, he wanted to fuck her.

He wanted her so badly even the spectacles gave him a raging hard-on.

"Jack!"

Jack's head snapped up. He smiled slowly as he watched John Calder take the thatched, twig-looking stairs two at a time, then stroll toward him. "How ya doin', buddy?"

John smiled fully, displaying perfectly even white teeth. He wiggled his eyebrows. "I've just finished conditioning the new women."

"Ah." Jack nodded as he swatted him affectionately on the back. "That explains the toothy grin then."

"Mmm," John agreed with another toothy grin. "There's one in particular—" He slanted an eyebrow at Jack. "A redhead I think you'll like."

Jack absently scratched his chin as he considered his friend's words. What better way to work off his lust over a redheaded witch than with another one. The logical part of him doubted this unknown woman would be as satisfying as seeing Professor Prickly submit to him, but as horny and surly as he was feeling, he'd take what he could get. For now.

Besides, it wasn't like his little witch would give him the time of day anyway.

Ack! Stop thinking about her, jackass! The whole point of coming here is to quit thinking about her, remember?

Jack absently ran a hand over his five o'clock shadow. "Sounds good, bud. But in the meantime I could use a shower and some sleep. I'm pretty beat."

John nodded. "You look like hell."

"Gee thanks," he growled.

He chuckled. "Come on and I'll show you to your hut. I reserved your favorite one for you."

Jack's eyebrow notched up. "Suddenly I'm feeling a hell of a lot better."

John laughed as he followed him up the stairs that resembled thatched twigs. "I don't blame you. Every voyeuristic pleasure a man could want and then some is viewable from that hut. But, unfortunately, the fun will have to wait until tomorrow. The new women are all being taken to the Massage Hut tonight to get them ready, and horny, for tomorrow."

Jack's attention was snagged by the opening thatched door of a nearby hut. He watched as a procession of five naked females, presumably all of them the new ones, were led from the Instruction Hut where they were given pointers on what was expected of them over the next five days and steered down a hall made to resemble a dirt floor. Jack had visited

John enough times to know that at the end of the dirt-packed hall was the Massage Hut, a place where the women's bodies would be rubbed and caressed by the young, muscular male help, further conditioning them to the touch of strangers.

Sometimes Jack found this entire place a bit overwhelming. It was true he was an old-fashioned, domineering, possessive kind of guy—and men like that by nature tended to think more of their own comfort than others—but Jack did think about others, and he wasn't the type who wanted an unwilling woman with him, no matter how well she was being paid for her submissiveness.

But hell, even John's own sister and business partner Sheri had chosen to work for hire at the resort once. She'd probably done it when she'd been in the mood for a little fun because she definitely didn't need the money. Far from it in fact. And the regulars around here had loved it when she'd chosen to work for hire because it was the only time any of them had gotten their hands on her.

Jack had never been with Sheri and never would. She was the one female in the world he truly felt was off limits to him because she was like the kid sister he'd never had. Plus John would kill him, he mused.

For as long as Jack lived he'd never figure out how it was that a man as protective of his younger sister as John was could let Sheri work for hire at the resort. Lord knows on the one occasion when she had, Jack had felt the protective urge to cover up her naked body and drag her back to the mainland where nobody here could touch her.

But Jack was Jack and John was John. Best friends they might be, but their personalities were worlds apart.

"There she is," John murmured, breaking him away from his thoughts. "Hot, isn't she?"

Jack's gaze honed in on the woman in question. Her back was to him as she walked away, but he had to agree that what he could see looked good. *Damn good.* With every swish of her full hips her dark red mane of curls bounced vibrantly, falling down her back and ending just above her round, lightly tanned ass. He felt his cock stiffen. "Very hot."

"I knew you'd like her," John said on a grin.

As Jack watched the sultry woman walk away, it occurred to him that her cascade of dark red hair was probably how his little witch's would look if she ever let it out of that deathly tight bun.

He found himself hoping that the redhead's face looked pert and intelligent like the professor's, then cursed himself for the fact that he wanted the prostitute to look like her at all.

"I want to massage her," Jack heard himself rumble out. It wasn't like him to not be able to wait, but there it was. He just wanted to know what she felt like...

John chuckled. "Consider it done."

* * * * *

The Massage Hut was an incredibly eye-opening experience for a woman whose most hedonistic pursuit to date, other than being conditioned by John, had taken place mostly in her fantasies.

"Let me see if I have this right," Kris whispered to the woman sitting next to her. The brunette's name was Elizabeth and she had worked one of these excursions before. "They are going to tie silk hoods over our heads so we can't see who's touching us?" She swallowed a bit roughly, feeling way out of her element.

Elizabeth grinned. "It's actually very pleasurable. The point of it is to teach your body to respond to touching — any touching — because not every man who touches you over the next five days will be handsome. Far from it, in fact," she said wryly.

She chewed that over for a long moment. She supposed she could see a glimmer of underlying logic to that, but...

Kris' face scrunched up. "Wouldn't it make more sense to not hood us and to have men of various states of attractiveness come in and touch us while we watched?" she asked, her scientific mind forever assessing and hypothesizing.

Elizabeth shrugged. "Probably. But hooding is the way it's done here so just lay back and enjoy." She grinned. "I think you'll enjoy it a lot more for your first night here than you would have had John brought in uggos to masturbate you."

She blew out a breath, conceding the point.

"Relax," Elizabeth said on a smile, patting her knee. "I promise you'll have a lot of fun."

And fun was why Kris was here. She smiled slowly, then nodded. "Consider me relaxed."

* * * * *

There she is.

Jack blew out a breath as he walked toward the padded lounger Red had been strapped down to. Her hands were bound above her head, her legs were tied apart spread-eagle and secured to posts, and her face was covered with a black silk hood. Still, he knew it was her. The dark red inverted triangle of pussy hair more or less gave her away.

Goddamn, he was hard.

And, he decided, he liked the black hood because without seeing her face he could pretend it was his little witch.

Jack didn't waste any time. He stared down at her body for no more than a few seconds before his calloused hands reached for her full breasts and palmed them.

He watched as her nipples immediately stiffened, stabbing up and wanting attention. He massaged them with the pads of his thumbs, his eyes hooded in arousal when a low moan escaped from behind the silk covering. "You like that, baby?" he asked thickly.

Oddly, her body stilled. But then, as if she'd thought something over and had decided to discard the idea altogether, she moaned out a yes.

Jack's gaze dropped to her exposed, puffed-up cunt. His eyes didn't have to fall far because the loungers had been raised up off of the ground so that they came about waist level on a guy his height. Presumably to make it comfortable for the massagers to touch the women without having to crouch down.

Unable to resist, he rubbed his steel-hard erection against the flesh of her pussy, softly groaning when he heard her low moan. When he backed up a step, his hand fell to his trousers and he immediately noted that they were wet with her arousal.

Jack's nostrils flared as one of his hands left her stiff nipples and began softly stroking her labial lips, rimming them in featherlight caresses.

Her body bucked up as best as it could on a moan, which was pretty far for a woman who'd been strapped down.

His jaw clenched as his thumb found her clit and he began working it around in slow, methodic circles.

She gasped, her back arching as if inviting him to fuck her.

Jack wanted to fuck her. Goddamn, how he wanted to. But he realized that tonight was reserved for strictly massaging, so he stifled the primitive urge to mount her like an animal in heat and settled for fondling her instead.

He rubbed her clit with more pressure, his cock stiffening until his balls ached, when he felt her dew saturate his hand. "I want to taste your cunt," he said hoarsely. He bent his head and drew the clit into the warmth of his mouth and suckled it. "Can I?" he mumbled after the fact from around the swollen piece of flesh.

She bucked up as if trying to smash her pussy into his face, her groans growing louder.

The Possession

"Good girl," he murmured. His calloused hands reached back up to massage her nipples, and his mouth clamped firmly onto her clit as he buried his face into her cunt...

Kris had never been more aroused in her life. Elizabeth had been correct; being hooded had much to recommend it. All of her senses were more alert from the blindfold, her sense of feel included.

This man whose face was buried between her legs—this man who had sounded like Jack McKenna of all people for one frightening moment!—well and truly knew how to eat a woman out. His throat made all these heady growling sounds as he lapped at her flesh, and she could hear the sound of him slurping up her clit and repeatedly suctioning it into his mouth.

"Oh," she breathed out, her back arching. She shivered when his thumbs began massaging her stiff nipples in methodic circles, flicking them back and forth, his lips and tongue driving her over the edge with the firm pressure being applied to her clit.

And then his face dove down on one of those sexy growls, and he sucked on her clit so hard she thought she was going to shatter into a million pieces. She moaned loudly, her nipples stabbing up to hit his thumbs as her lower body began involuntarily shaking.

"Yes."

She came on a hysterical groan, mumbling incoherently as she arched her back and thrust her swollen flesh into his face as though she wanted him to devour her. Blood rushed to heat her face and made her nipples stiffen to the point of aching. Her vaginal walls contracted as she came hard and violently.

He growled against her pussy like a dog with a bone, refusing to relinquish her clit. She was already sensitive from having orgasmed, so the painful pleasure of the pressure made her scream. He sucked harder and harder still, slurping up her clit and suckling it until she thought she might go insane.

"No more!" she begged.

But he didn't listen. He sucked on her clit harder, taking her to a place she'd never before been because she'd always stopped after the first orgasm made her feel ultra-sensitive.

When she came this time it was so hard she saw stars. "*Oh god.*" Her buttocks reared up as if offering him all the pussy he wanted. "*Yes.*"

It was another fifteen minutes and two violent orgasms before his appetite for cunt eating was satiated. When his face finally left her drenched flesh, and after he spent a few solid minutes sucking on her nipples like lollipops, he petted her glistening dark red triangle, his calloused fingers running through the soft curls as if he owned them.

"Good girl," he murmured, praising her physical response to him.

And then he was gone.

A long moment passed in stark quiet.

Kris blew out a breath, grinning from behind the black silk hood. She wished she'd seen his face because she was certain she had just fallen in love.

Chapter Four

Still naked, and disallowed the use of clothing for the next five days, Kris stared at herself in the full-length mirror housed within the large hut she was sharing with the other four newbies, plus three more women who had worked an island excursion or two before.

She simply couldn't believe it, but her new friend Elizabeth had been right. She truly did look like a different woman with makeup on. "Wow."

Elizabeth chuckled as she strolled up behind her. "Told you so." She grinned at her in the mirror. "You look gorgeous, Krissy."

Kris' body stilled as she thought something over. "Do you think I should go by an alias here? I mean, what if it gets back to the university that—"

"Honestly, I wouldn't worry about it," the statuesque brunette assured her. "Nobody here would dare breathe a word about it because in order to do so they'd have to admit how they saw you here in the first place." She scooted in next to her and began applying some flavored lip balm to Kris' lips with her index finger. "Trust me. None of the men who come here would risk their necks like that." She grinned. "Great, ain't it?"

Kris snorted at that, agreeing when she thought back on the man who had licked her half insane last night. She smacked her lips together and smoothed out the balm. "Mmm. Tastes like coconut."

"Yeah, I love it." Elizabeth applied the balm to her own lips and smacked them together to even it out. "Almost like a piña colada."

"Speaking of piña coladas, do we ever get some rest and relaxation time around here during the next five days?" She smiled. "You know, some time away from the men to be with just the girls when you get sick of being submissive?"

Elizabeth chuckled as she began applying flavored coconut oil to her nipples. She passed the small vial off to Kris for her to use as she began working the sweet-smelling stuff in. "Definitely. Tonight when all the in-house bars close down at three in the morning we'll get a chance to unwind together. That's kind of nice. Just like the massages it helps you prepare yourself for the big night to come tomorrow."

Kris nodded. In the Instruction Hut she had been brought up to speed on how the five-day excursion worked. Tonight, the first night, the cardinal rule was no sex allowed. John permitted the male patrons to touch and fondle the women, but that was as far as they were allowed to take it. Sheri had called it Foreplay Day, and had explained with a grin that by the time night three rolled around the men would be so horny for the women's services that they'd pay extra hefty prices for the pleasure of having them.

But Kris didn't care about the money. She wanted the sex.

She was nervous about tonight without a doubt, but was also looking forward to it more than she'd ever anticipated anything in her life.

"What happens on day two again?" Kris asked as she worked the coconut oil into her own nipples.

"Day two is Exploration Day," Elizabeth reminded her as she leaned in close to the mirror to apply mascara. "On Exploration Day the men compete in contests—kinda like the ones at a state fair. Except at this fair, all the contest prizes are women—us," she clarified. "Days three, four, and five are all called Submission Days," she continued. "On day three you are given to whichever master paid the steepest price for you at auction and you're his to do with as he will until the excursion is over."

Kris' brow wrinkled in thought as she watched her apply the mascara. "Do a lot of the men pay to 'own' more than one woman?"

Elizabeth shrugged as she set down the mascara and picked up the eyeliner. "It depends on the guy and what he's into. Some of them purchase three or four women and some of them are content to have one. Some guys like the intimacy of spending three days and nights with one slave, while others prefer a cooler, less personal relationship with several."

"Huh. Interesting."

Elizabeth grinned at her in the mirror. "It really is. By the time you leave here you'll know more about the male psyche than you ever wanted to."

Kris snorted at that. She folded her arms under her breasts as she absently watched Elizabeth finish applying the remainder of her makeup. "So what do you do in real life?"

Elizabeth glanced at her from over her shoulder. "I teach the third grade if you can believe it."

Kris grinned, a dimple showing in either cheek. "I'm an anthropologist."

Elizabeth grinned back, chuckling. "Expect to have your site thoroughly excavated."

* * * * *

An hour later, and after a fainter coconut oil than the rich oil that had been applied to her nipples had been worked into the rest of her body, Kris left the safety of the communal hut and followed the other women to the third floor where they would be serving drinks in various assorted tiki bars on the premises.

Totally nude and her body exotically oiled down, the feel of cool air hitting naked skin left her feeling decidedly aroused. The gentle jiggle that her breasts made as she walked to the third floor sensitized her nipples until they were stiff and swollen.

She could feel her heart pounding against her chest in cold, stark fear. And yet, conversely, she could also feel her clit swelling between her legs in hot, unadulterated anticipation.

This is as far from being a good girl as you can get, Kris. Savor every second of these five days because you can never chance returning to this island. It's far too risky.

The sound of gregarious male laughter and voices reached her ears. It wafted through the air, mingling with the tangy aroma of cigar smoke, the sweet scent of tropical fruits, and the expensive smell of gourmet food. It sounded as though the men had already scattered throughout the third floor, all of them in various tiki huts being served food and drink.

She wet her lips. "Who is serving them meals?" she whispered to Elizabeth, wide-eyed.

Elizabeth glanced toward her, her dark eyes as round as Kris' green ones. "The women who regularly work these excursions. They know they are less likely to be sold at auction because they are familiar to the men, so they vie for the waitressing jobs to make huge tips that way."

Kris nodded. She could see Elizabeth's nervousness as if it was a tangible thing—a fact that helped to calm her, as well as bond her even closer to the other woman. She threaded her fingers through hers. "It'll be okay," she murmured. "We're going to have a good time. Try to remember that."

Elizabeth squeezed her hand like a vice-grip. "I know," she said in a rush. "But the anticipation is about to give me heart failure. I just want to get it over with so to speak."

Kris smiled. "I know what you mean. I feel like my heart is going to thump right out of my chest. But we're almost there," she whispered. "Once we see the men and they are no longer faceless unknown creatures to us it'll be easier to deal with this rather overwhelming situation."

Elizabeth half snorted and half laughed. "I'm the one who's been here before. It should be me calming you."

Kris chuckled softly, squeezing her hand one last time before letting it drop. "You'll get your turn." She was afraid if they walked into the tiki hut together with threaded hands the men would assume they had been sent in to put on a lesbian show for them. She didn't think she was quite ready for that much. Two days ago, after all, she'd been sitting at home watching the History Channel with her five cats.

Well this is it, she thought breathlessly as they finished walking up the dirt-packed ramp and rounded a corner. *Another ten seconds and I'll be strolling into one of the tiki huts totally naked in front of a bunch of strange men.*

Ten seconds later she did just that.

Chapter Five
༜

The sound of catcalls, of wealthy, spoiled men whistling through their teeth, caused Jack to glance up from his meal.

There they were—the new girls. And Red was with them.

Goddamn, she looked good, he thought. Maybe she'd help him get the witch out of his mind after all.

He thought back on last night, on how delicious her cunt had tasted, on how plump and perfect for sucking her nipples were, and felt his cock begin to stir from the confines of his expensive black trousers.

It would help if you quit pretending she's your witch, he thought glumly. *Maybe if you quit pretending you'd be able to enjoy her for herself and not as a stand-in.*

Jack set down his fork and cleared his throat as he leaned back on the thatched twig chair that had been padded with French silk pillowing. He was seated on the far side of the tiki-torch lit bar, so he knew the women would have to stroll by him in order to meet his buddy John up at the bar proper to be given their table assignments.

He couldn't wait to get a load of her face.

He couldn't wait to get a load in her, period.

Jack's eyes narrowed at a French millionaire named Lauren Thibauld when the handsome playboy snatched Red out of the line-up as she walked by and stood her before his seat. She gasped when the millionaire palmed her breasts and began kneading them like two large balls of dough.

Although she was standing in profile to him, her dark red curls concealing half of her face, a weird spark of familiarity induced Jack's brow to scrunch up. There was something too familiar about her—about her height, about the way she stood, about the size of her full breasts...

Nah. She just reminded him of his witch was all.

He sighed. *Quit thinking about her!*

"Ah, there she is." John chuckled as he strolled up behind him and patted Jack on the back. "Popular with the boys already I see."

Jack grunted. "You better tell Frenchy to back the hell off," he growled. "I don't share and I want her."

John's eyebrows rose in feigned surprise. "Do tell." He sighed. "To be honest, Jack, I was hoping Lauren wouldn't take an interest in her. I knew you'd want her the moment I saw her and, well, Lauren is one hell of a high bidder."

Jack's jaw clenched as he watched the millionaire's hand delve between Red's legs to stroke her clit. "I'll outbid him."

John chuckled at his arrogance. "For now I'm going to break this little groping session up so I can give the women their table assignments." He waited for Jack to meet his gaze before adding, "But from there you're on your own, my friend. Understand that I can't break the rules for even you or none of the others will want to patronize the resort again."

Jack nodded, but said nothing. He didn't need John's help anyway. He was having Red to himself and that was that.

He didn't share. Ever.

Kris didn't know if she should feel relieved or disappointed when John Calder approached Mr. Thibauld's table and good-naturedly informed him that he'd have to save his fondling until after she'd been given her table assignment.

Lauren Thibauld was a bit unskilled with his hands, but on the other hand he was quite handsome and not all of the men here were, she'd quickly surmised. If she was going to be the personal sex slave of a man for three days, which she most definitely wanted to be, then she would prefer for the man to be as good-looking as possible.

And so with mixed emotions she allowed John to steer her away from the Frenchman's table, knowing the separation would allow enough time for one of the women who frequently worked the island excursions to try to entice him away from her in lieu of themselves.

She was right. The very moment she was led away, his lap was filled up with two naked women dotting his face with quick kisses and squeezing his erect cock through his trousers.

Kris sighed. She glanced away, her gaze absently raking the hut while she followed John toward the bar with the other women.

As she strolled through the bar, her nude body oiled up to give it a sleek, exotic appearance, she felt a very strange, and yet very familiar premonition pass over her. That same premonition she'd had yesterday when Jack McKenna had followed her into her office.

That feeling of being watched.

That feeling of being hunted.

When she turned her head a bit to the left, when her face was no longer in profile to the patrons seated toward the back table nearest the bar, Kris' heart rate sped up to the point of almost fainting and her eyes widened in shock and disbelief as she beheld a sight she had never thought to see.

Jack McKenna.

Here, at Hotel Atlantis.

Oh. My. God.

At first she didn't think he recognized her, for although his dark eyes were raking over her in an aroused fashion, no comprehension seemed to dwell in them. His brooding gaze devoured her oiled up breasts, stared lingeringly at the thatch of dark red curls at the juncture of her thighs…

Then he did a double take. His eyes widened. And then she saw his jaw go slack.

"Oh. My. God," he murmured as she strolled by his table.

Her thoughts exactly.

And then she heard him laugh. A deep, booming, victorious laugh.

Suddenly, she missed her cats.

Chapter Six

Jack was pissed.

When he'd first realized that Red and Professor Prickly were one and the same, he'd been shocked. Then he'd been aroused by the memories of eating her out and making her orgasm last night, not to mention damn near euphoric knowing he wasn't going to have to settle for buying a woman who looked like his witch, but instead would get the real deal.

But now he was pissed. Goddamn pissed. For a combination of reasons.

First of all, it irritated him to no end to realize that for the past two years he'd been pining away for a woman who had let him know in no uncertain terms through her holier-than-thou pompous tones and attitude that she was too good for him, only to find out she'd been for sale to the highest bidder all along.

No, no, that couldn't be right, he qualified with a frown. She was new here, so obviously this was her first time, but...why then?

Why was she working for John?

He stilled.

John. John, his best friend who had masturbated her, he thought angrily, his heart rate speeding up.

Sweet Jesus, that better have been all the man had done.

And there she was on the other side of the tiki hut serving drinks to every man but him. Jack was forced to sit at his table and do nothing while he watched a bunch of spoiled men who'd been born with silver spoons in their mouths grope and fondle her. With every moment that passed by he grew angrier

The Possession

and angrier—and more determined to be the highest bidder at the auction. If he had to watch one more goddamn man run his hands over her sweet ass...

She had been assigned to work the table he was seated at, but he had heard her beg John to give her another one. Any table, she had said. Any table but his.

Worse yet, John had backed down and complied, leaving Jack pissed off at him too. He felt like he was purposely being toyed with, the way his supposed best friend had dangled Kris Torrence in front of him like a piece of candy and then snatched her away. He was being toyed with and he wasn't the type of man to take insult lightly.

Of course, he conceded, John didn't know that Red was his witch.

"Last call," a naked busty blonde named Barbi cheerfully called out from the bar. "Closing time is in ten minutes."

Jack glanced away as a drunken patron reached for Barbi's big breasts and dove his face into them with a groan while she giggled. He checked his watch. Two-fifty a.m.

Ten more minutes and John and the women would retire to a private bar to wind down for the evening. He'd make sure he was invited.

For the next ten minutes Jack sat in his seat, his eyes angrily narrowed at the sweet ass he refused to look away from. With every hand he saw touch it, with every set of eyes that grazed over her naked, oiled body, his possessiveness increased until he felt ready to explode.

Tomorrow was Exploration Day. He'd be on her like white on rice to make sure no man but him touched her.

The next day he could buy her. And she'd be all his.

While he waited for the ten minutes to pass, he thought up the various things he would do to her when that body belonged to him.

All of the things he hadn't been able to do in the Massage Hut.

* * * * *

By the time three a.m. rolled around, Kris was tired and weary. She'd tried to enjoy all the sensual touching she'd experienced, but much to her dismay she hadn't. She could only assume her lack of interest in the hedonism going on around her was due to *him*.

The Grinch.

She nibbled on her lower lip as she and Elizabeth followed the others to a remote, first floor tiki bar to unwind from the crazy atmosphere that had permeated the evening. Would Jack McKenna rat her out to the university, she wondered? The very worry of it made her stomach knot until she felt like she might vomit.

Her entire life as she knew it was about to end. She would lose her tenure, if not her job altogether, and be forced to retire in disgrace.

And all because she had wanted to bring a little bit of excitement into her life.

Elizabeth had assured her that none of the men here would rat her out because in order to do so they would have to admit they'd been to Hotel Atlantis, but clearly Elizabeth had never dealt with Jack McKenna before. The big bruiser wouldn't care who knew he'd been to Hotel Atlantis. In fact, she thought glumly, he'd probably be proud of it. Sort of like a notch on the bedpost.

When she arrived at the bar, the first thing she did was take a deep breath. The second thing she did was down the piña colada Elizabeth had handed off to her in less than a minute.

"Sheesh! That was quick." Elizabeth grinned. "Care for another?"

Kris sighed. She smiled when John walked by and handed her another piña colada, then turned back to Elizabeth who was standing up leaning against the bar just like she was.

Her eyes absently flicked over Elizabeth's perfect, naked body. It was strange, she thought, but it hadn't taken her long to accustom herself to total nudity. Once she had been out there in front of the men and exposed to them, she had quit feeling shy in less than ten minutes.

"I'm having one hell of a bad night," Kris confessed. She saluted her friend with the tropical drink, and then proceeded to sip from it.

Elizabeth's face scrunched up. "Why? I saw that Frenchman all over you and he is so damn hot." She playfully nudged her in the shoulder and smiled. "Bet he bids on you."

"Bet he doesn't win."

Kris froze at the sound of that very familiar, and very surly, masculine voice speaking directly from behind her. Instinctually, she set her drink down on the bar and covered her breasts and mons as best as she could, then turned around to face her nemesis.

Jack rolled his eyes. "A little late for modesty, ain't it, professor?"

Elizabeth's eyes widened. "He called you professor," she murmured. "He knows…" She stopped abruptly. "Oh shit," she muttered.

Kris took a deep breath. Her thoughts exactly.

"Come here," Jack said in a would-broach-no-argument tone. "Now."

Kris' first instinct was to straighten her spine and tell him what he could do with his growled out commands like she always did, but she was too tired and too upset to argue with him. Besides, she wanted to find out what his intentions were. If he was going to get her fired, she needed some mental prep time.

"Fine," she said weakly, her hands still covering her breasts and mons as best they could. "Where?"

Jack grunted. Rather than answer her, he took her by the arm and gently guided her to the far end of the bar and away from curious eyes. When he was sure they were out of earshot from the others, he whirled her around to face him. She was still covering herself, her hands shielding her private parts from him.

He rolled his eyes again and tore her hands away from her body. With a warning growl he planted them firmly at her sides. "Do not," he bit out, "shield yourself from me." His nostrils flared as he got his first good look at her nude, oiled down body up close and personal. Well, the first good look he'd had at it once he'd been aware of the fact that it belonged to the Prickly Professor and not to just any old prostitute. "Lord knows you haven't bothered shielding yourself from anyone else."

She sighed, too tired to care if he looked his fill at her or not. "Are you going to get me fired?" she asked bluntly, coming straight to the point. "Is that why you brought me over here? To gloat?" Her body stiffened. "Because if it is, save yourself the trouble. I already figured out the moment I saw you that I'd need to look for a new job as soon as I return to San Francisco." She said the words boldly, but was pretty sure even a man as insensitive as Jack McKenna could hear the trembling in her voice.

His eyes softened a bit, surprising her. "Hell no I'm not gonna get you fired! Jesus, I'm not that bad, lady," he said gruffly.

She stilled, not certain as to whether or not he could be believed. Then again, Jack McKenna was an in-your-face kind of man. She doubted he was the type to give her hope about something so serious and then go back on his word. If he wanted to rat her out, he'd be gloating over it, not acting all surly over the fact that she had thought he'd do something like that to her to begin with.

That in and of itself confused her. Why did he care what she thought of him anyway?

They locked gazes, dark brooding eyes meeting worried cat-like green ones.

The Possession

"Why are you here?" Jack murmured. He placed his large, calloused hands on her shoulders and began to gently knead them. His dark eyes softened for a fraction of a second before resuming their normal level of steel. "Do you need money, sweetheart?"

Perversely, the fact that after two years of grunting and growling at her Jack McKenna was trying in his surly, patronizing way to be nice to her, made her feel like crying. Between that and the fact that she was exhausted and had experienced so many extreme emotions today, her eyes teared up for just a second. She cleared her throat, blinked them away, and answered him truthfully.

"No," she admitted. She glanced away for a second and sighed, then looked back at him. "Listen, Mr. McKenna..."

"Jack," he growled.

"Jack," she conceded. She sighed again. "I really appreciate the fact that you're trying to help, but I don't need any money." She took a deep breath. "I'm doing this for me," she said quietly. "Not for money."

That dark eyebrow shot up, though this time out of confusion and not to irritate her. "I don't follow."

She closed her eyes briefly, expelling a shaky breath as she did so. When she opened them again, she explained how she felt as best she could given how tired and bone weary she felt. "I'm getting older, Jack. Not old, but older." She shrugged her shoulders, which he was still kneading, and glanced away. "I wanted to do something wild and crazy just once in my life. For as long as I've lived and breathed I've followed the rules, as you know and like to belittle me for all the time, and..." She felt his body still at the truth as she glanced back to him. "And for once I didn't feel like following them anymore."

"But why here?" he asked, still not quite getting it. "I can understand the wanting to do something wild and crazy part, but I don't get why you wanted to—"

He stopped abruptly, his dark eyes widening in dawning comprehension, and then narrowing in arousal.

He stared at her, his cock as hard as a rock, his heavy-lidded eyes studying her lips. "You like the submissive part, don't you, baby?" he asked huskily.

Kris wet her lips and looked away. When he called her pet names like that it did things to her it shouldn't. Like harden her nipples and make her clit pulse. "Maybe," she squeaked. She cleared her throat. "Maybe."

"Maybe my ass," he murmured. His hands fell from her shoulders, trailed down her back, and palmed her buttocks as he drew her in closer. She sucked in a surprised breath, but didn't try to push him away.

Goddamn, Jack thought, he was horny as hell.

All these years he'd been trying to find a woman who was submissive in general, catering to his every whim, but had grown quickly bored by each and every one of them. He didn't know why he'd been looking for that, but conceded it probably had something to do with his assertive, independent ex. She had walked all over him, cheated on him, used him—and he'd been devastated. So after their marriage had broken up, he'd gone looking for her antithesis.

He'd found plenty of them. But although he'd enjoyed that submissiveness on a sexual level, those women had bored him to tears on all other levels.

As it turned out, what he'd really wanted all along was a free-thinking woman like Dr. Kris Torrence. An independent, infuriating woman who would give as good as she got out of the bedroom, but who would also worship him and his cock inside of the bedroom, or wherever he wanted the bedroom to be.

He hadn't realized this facet of his personality until a few seconds ago. Until the woman he'd had more masturbation sessions fantasizing about than he could count had more or less admitted she craved to be sexually dominated. And he had his submissive little witch right here in his arms...

"I want you, Krissy," he said thickly, his large hands kneading her buttocks as he pressed his erection against her bare belly. He wanted to get as naked as she was. "I've wanted you for a long, long time."

Her eyes flew up to meet his. "And I've wanted y—" She abruptly stopped her confession, and then looked away. Her heartbeat sped up, thumping madly. "Jack," she breathed out. "We can't do this. It's best if you leave me alone. I see you at work all the time even if we rarely speak," she said in a rush of emotion and tripped over words. "How can I pretend like nothing ever happened when I see you? I'm not so cold as that—"

"I don't want you to be cold," he interrupted, his voice thick with arousal. He ground his erection, concealed through the fabric of his black Italian trousers, against her belly again. "The last thing I want from you, sweetheart, is cold."

Kris was about to open her mouth and argue, but was given no time. Jack's mouth came down on top of hers, firmly, demandingly, broaching no argument, as he thrust his tongue between her lips.

She whimpered a bit—in defeat, or in admission of her attraction to him she couldn't say. But she didn't even bother to try to fight him. Lord knows she'd secretly wondered a million times what his kisses felt and tasted like and now she knew the answer. Paradise.

On a low moan, Kris wrapped her arms around his neck and buried her hands into his silky black hair. He picked her up on a growl, slanting his mouth over hers again and again as he possessively branded her with his kisses.

Carrying her to a remote, out of view table, he sat down on a padded thatched twig chair and set her atop him so that she straddled his lap.

Both of them breathing heavily, he tore his mouth away from hers, his hands firmly clutching her buttocks. "Touch him," he said hoarsely, his eyes heavy-lidded. "Unzip my pants and touch him."

Kris drew in a ragged breath to steady her breathing. Her breasts heaved up and down as she sat atop him divested of clothing and slicked down with coconut oil. She could still scarcely believe she was sitting naked in Jack McKenna's lap. And that he wanted her to touch him.

She hesitated for a few seconds, long enough to make herself feel as though she'd at least attempted to resist, but then her hands flew to his fly and began unzipping them. She could see how labored his breathing was—proof that he wanted her—and it made her all the more frantic to masturbate him. This man, her nemesis, had been the subject of more fantasies than even she could remember. And now at last she would know what the erect penis she had repeatedly fantasized about looked like.

Her eyes narrowed in desire as she wrapped her hand around the thick length of him. He groaned at the contact, squeezing her buttocks with his palms and thrusting his hips up to grind his manhood against her hand.

His cock was glorious. Unlike the medium-tan rest of him, his long penis was a light tan, ruby-red at the tip, and the thickest she'd ever seen. She ran a finger over the large vein that ran the length of it, pumping blood into his huge manhood. "It's beautiful," she whispered, her voice aroused.

She heard him groan.

"Touch him," he told her thickly, his dark eyes narrowed in desire. "Make him cum, Krissy."

She decided she liked it when he called her by that name. It felt intimate and special...and it was a name no man had ever called her by but Jack.

Wrapping her hand firmly around the base of his cock, she slowly began to masturbate him, for once reveling in the growling sounds he made instead of frowning at them.

"Faster, baby," he gritted out, perspiration dotting his brow. He brought his rough hands around the front of her and slowly slid the palms up and down her breasts, all over her swollen nipples. "Hard and fast," he said thickly.

She did as he'd ordered her to do, masturbating him hard and fast. The feel of his rock-hard, silky smooth penis in her hand was a turn-on, as was the feel of his palms grazing over her nipples.

Her other hand reached between them and massaged the tight balls. She rolled them around between her fingers until he groaned.

"Do you like that?" she murmured, feeling headily powerful as she pumped him with one hand and massaged him with the other. "Or do you need to sink it into my pussy?"

Jack came on a loud groan, the mere mention of being inside of her sending him over the edge. He gritted his teeth as he violently spurted, leaning back against the chair and moaning when he watched her try to catch some of his hot semen with her mouth. "Jesus," he muttered. "You're gonna be a handful, sweetheart. But I like that."

Kris lapped up his salty sperm, loving that she at last knew what it tasted like. Later, she was certain she would freak out—later, when it dawned on her how wicked and brazen she had behaved with Jack McKenna—and with very little prompting on his part. But for now...

She smiled when her face at last bobbed up into his line of vision. She swallowed the semen she had caught with her mouth in front of him, letting him watch the intimate, sensuous act.

He gulped, his Adam's apple working up and down. She grinned.

"Witch," he muttered. "Redheaded witch." His gaze trailed down to the thatch of trimmed, dark red curls between her thighs. "All real and all mine while you're here," he murmured as he ran his fingers through it.

She shivered, gasping when his thumb found her clit and began rubbing it. She held on to his shoulders as he intimately massaged her, her hips slowly undulating to get more friction.

He rubbed her faster, brisker, causing her to moan.

"Cum for me," he said thickly, his thumb expertly rubbing the wet and swollen piece of female flesh. She gasped when two fingers on his other hand penetrated her, sinking deep into her pussy. "Ride me, baby," he murmured.

She groaned as she rode his fingers, fucking herself with them as fast as she could while he rubbed her clit, her heavy breasts bouncing up and down before him. She gasped when his mouth latched onto a nipple with a growl and frantically sucked on it.

She rode his fingers faster and faster, bouncing up and down on top of them, her eyes closed while she moaned, her body screaming with the need to orgasm.

His mouth sucked hard on her nipple, his fingers remained buried deep inside of her flesh, his thumb continued to firmly rub her clit.

"Oh my god."

She gyrated her hips frantically as she burst, riding his fingers as fast as she could while she drenched his hand. He released her nipple with a popping sound, then sat back and watched her come, his dark eyes narrowed in arousal as he felt her vaginal muscles tremble around his fingers.

When it was done, when she had come down from her orgasmic high, she could do nothing but breathe heavily and cling to him, his fingers still buried possessively inside of her.

He stroked her ass with his free hand, murmuring to her in his rough voice about what a good girl she'd been.

Long moments later, when both of them were calm, Jack peeled her torso off of his so he could make eye contact with her. His dark eyes were serious, brooding. His drenched, calloused fingers left her vagina, then trailed up to play in her glistening triangle of dark red curls. "Don't let another man on the island touch your cunt," he warned her. "I mean it, Krissy. I couldn't handle it."

Kris closed her eyes briefly and took a calming breath. "Jack..."

"Don't try to get me jealous," he said softly. Too softly. "It's called playing with fire, sweetheart. And you know what happens to bad girls who play with fire."

They get burned.

The words hung there between them, unspoken.

She sighed. "Jack, it's not that I want to be with another man in particular on the island, but realistically, don't you think we should stay away from each other? I mean, what happens when we return to the real world? The more that passes between us here, the weirder the situation will be."

He opened his mouth to speak, but she forestalled him when she gently pressed her palm to his lips. "Don't do this," she said almost desperately as she crawled out of his lap.

This was just too much. She was tired and overwhelmed and confused and—

Kris released his mouth as she rose to her feet. Her nostrils flared as she stood naked and defiant before him. "I won't fall for you, Jack McKenna. I won't do it!" She blew out a breath and shook her head slightly. "Please just stay away from me," she whispered.

And with that she turned around and fled from the tiki bar.

His mouth agape, Jack watched her sweet ass walk quickly away from him. Until the moment she'd spoken the betraying words, he'd had no idea that Professor Prickly had been carrying around a flame for him that could rival the torch he'd been carrying around for her.

One side of his mouth lifted in an awkward smile.

Leave her alone?

Hell, he'd only just begun.

Chapter Seven

༄

Feeling a bit depressed, Kris applied the rich coconut oil into her nipples as she prepared for Exploration Day. The name was kind of a misnomer, she idly considered, since Exploration Day didn't commence until nine o'clock at night.

Well, whatever it should have been called, she conceded, didn't really matter. She just wanted it over and done with.

She'd spent most of the day sleeping and the rest of it worrying over tonight. Before last night, before Jack, she would have looked forward to having a bunch of wild sexual forays with complete strangers. It was why she had come here after all.

Maybe. She wasn't so sure of anything anymore.

Least of all, Jack.

After he'd touched her the way he had last night, and after she had touched him the way she had, it dawned on her that perhaps she hadn't wanted to come to Hotel Atlantis just for the sake of being wild and crazy. Perhaps she had wanted to come to Hotel Atlantis to prove to herself that she could be as sexy as all the brainless bimbos Jack had dated in the two years she'd known him. The very realization of such a thought had panicked her enough to run away from him.

Jack! Jack! Jack! Why did it always come back to the Grinch? she thought with a harrumph.

He was the bane of her existence, she decided on a martyr's sigh.

But bane of her existence or not, he was also the sole star of every fevered fantasy she'd entertained in the past two years. And the only man on earth who could get her wet just by growling, she thought grimly.

Kris straightened her shoulders as she gazed at herself in the mirror. She had been hired for this five-day island excursion to do a job, she reminded herself. A job that she had very badly wanted to undertake. John was depending on her to fulfill her obligations and live up to her word.

And besides, she truly did want to experience submission with a man, to live out her deepest sexual fantasies with a handsome, domineering male.

Unfortunately, she frowned, the only man she could imagine ordering her around a bedroom was and had always been Jack McKenna.

But after the frightened tantrum she'd thrown last night, it was quite possible that Jack wouldn't bid on her.

Stop it, Kris! Would you quit it with the Jack thoughts already! The man has loathed you for two years and now, because he masturbated you, you're stupidly romantic enough to hope his feelings have changed? Yeah right! Besides, she tried to convince herself, *he's all wrong for you.*

Kris took a deep breath and blew it out.

She had been hired by John Calder as a high paid prostitute for five hedonistic days. She had a job to do.

And she had less than an hour to talk herself into enjoying it.

* * * * *

Sheri Calder Conner Carucci turned around slowly in her swivel seat office chair to face her older brother. Her eyes wide, she simply gawked at him.

"What?" John grunted. He blushed, looking away.

She blinked several times in rapid succession. "Getting a little sentimental in your advanced years, Johnny?"

He threw her a "yeah right" look then strolled to the other side of the office and poured a glass of bourbon.

"Gut rot," she said in an absent monotone as she tried to work him out in her mind. "Shouldn't drink the stuff."

When he said nothing, when he just stood there absently staring out the seventh floor window, Sheri stood up and slowly walked toward him. "Always trying to be the hero," she murmured. "But then that's what I love about you."

He snorted at that. "I've never been a hero to anyone. Least of all to you—"

"Yes, you were," she interrupted, wrapping her arms around his waist from behind and pressing her cheek against his back. "We didn't choose to have the childhood we did, John, but there it is. And you protected me from it better than any other twelve-year-old boy ever could have."

"But it wasn't enough," he said unblinkingly. "It simply wasn't enough."

"Hey I resent that!" She chuckled as she turned him around to face her. "Listen, I've got my faults but overall I'm a pretty decent woman." She waited for him to look at her before continuing. "Okay so I picked the wrong guys twice, married them twice, and divorced them twice. But other than that," she shrugged, "I've got it all. I'm happy, Johnny. I'm very, very happy. And," she said, thumping him on the chest, "I owe it all to you, you big idiot."

When his forehead wrinkled and he opened his mouth to speak, she could tell he was going to counter her admission with a rebuttal. She groaned, thumping him again. "Stop it! My shitty marriages didn't have anything to do with you. There was nothing you could have done to stop me from marrying the wrong guys." That wasn't entirely true, but now wasn't the time to bring up old ghosts. "It just happens. To lots of women," she said pointedly. "Not just women whose parents beat the living shit out of them as kids."

He sighed as he swiped a hand over his jaw.

"Let it go," she said softly. "Because there's not a damn thing wrong with me." That wasn't completely true either. She did carry one secret that weighed down on her pretty heavily. But, sadly, she'd come to realize it was a secret she would have to take to her grave.

His nostrils flared as he looked away, staring out into the night.

She sighed as she ran her hand up and down his back in a soothing gesture. "Have you ever considered the possibility that maybe, just maybe, you sequester yourself away on a remote island with a bunch of naked women because it's easier than going out on an emotional limb with just one?"

He grunted. "Tell me something I don't know."

She clucked her tongue. "Try being your own hero for a change. I can take care of myself. And so can Jack."

He sighed, then turned to her and grinned in an effort to change the subject. "I don't know that I'm ready for such a monumental step for myself. However, we are in a position to help Jack out with Kris."

"I like her," Sheri said simply. "There's just something solid about her, know what I mean?"

John nodded. "I don't want you to give her any of the assignments tonight that could possibly end in fucking. That way if Jack loses any of the contests—"

"Jack?" she interrupted with a chuckle. "Not Jack. Let's remember he's not one of those soft rich boys down there, my dear. This is Jack we're talking about. Just like you, he's had to fight for everything he's ever had tooth and nail."

"Which makes him appreciate it more than they do," he said softly, his gaze turning back to the window.

"Exactly." Sheri thought the problem over for a moment, then nodded when the solution came to her. "I can pay Cherice off, get her to come down with a sudden case of the flu, and tell Kris I need her to wait tables at one of the tiki huts tonight instead of—"

"No."

"No?" Her brow furrowed. "I thought you wanted to make sure Kris doesn't end up in bed with any of the men tonight."

"That is what I want."

"Then...?"

"I only want you to give her assignments that can go no further than groping, fondling, and oral. That way if Jack loses any of the contests, he won't be forced to watch her fuck another man."

Sheri groaned. "Why go through all the subterfuge? Why not just pull her out of the line-up altogether?"

John raised the bourbon to his lips and sipped it as he stared out into the night. He sighed, relishing the burn as it glided down his throat. "Because I want him to have to work for her," he murmured. "I want him to sweat all night long, wondering if she's going to be the prize at a contest where the winner gets all." He set the glass down. "I want him to go through hell and back mentally before the auction tomorrow. Because..."

"Because it will make him appreciate her more," she softly finished.

"Yes."

Sheri smiled. "This is so cool, Johnny. Maybe we should think about tearing this place down and opening a Fantasy Island to bring lovers together," she quipped.

John chuckled as he turned his head to look down at her. "Okay. But you get to be Tattoo."

She laughed and threw him a "yeah right" look before turning on her heel to leave. "Sheri Calder Conner Carucci is officially on the case," she threw over her shoulder as she reached the door. She stopped before she opened it. "Oh and one more thing, Johnny," she said, her face turning to the left so she could make eye contact with him.

He raised an eyebrow but said nothing.
"You're my hero," she murmured.
She left before he could reply.

Chapter Eight

Jack was delirious with panic as he looked for Krissy. All sorts of gut-wrenching scenarios went through his mind about the kinds of contests she was liable to be the prize in. But the worst one, he knew, was *Pin the Dick in the Pussy*, so it was to that booth he went first. When he quickly surmised that his professor wasn't to be the prize at that contest, that some other woman would get screwed by the winner, he left immediately and searched the grounds for the right booth.

The surrounding courtyard of Hotel Atlantis was massive and dimly lit, the only light that was given off by blazing tiki torches. Much like a state fair, contest booths were set up all over it, only many of the games were x-rated and the prizes were gorgeous, naked women.

To the right of him was a pussy-eating contest, and to the left of him was the rubber ducky booth. The rubber ducky booth was set up the same way it was at state fairs where contestants got to choose one rubber ducky out of a dozen or so that were swimming by and pick it up to see what he'd won. Only instead of the prizes being stuffed animals, the bottoms of the duckies said things like "a blowjob" or "five minutes of cunt licking".

Jack jogged by the rubber ducky booth, paying an angry customer no attention when he started yelling he'd been cheated out of his money because the bottom of his ducky said "a kiss".

"Where are you?" he muttered to himself, his panic and possessiveness growing steeper with every passing moment. He continued jogging by various assorted booths, his heart rate increasing. "Where the hell—"

"*Sitting spread out on the stage for your viewing pleasure,*" a loud, disembodied male voice boomed out through a microphone, "*we have the slut Krissy...*"

Jack's eyes narrowed first at the word slut and then at the name Krissy. "Don't call her that, asshole. And don't call her by my pet name for her either," he gritted out as he picked up the speed of his jogging.

"*As you can see our horny little Krissy is a natural redhead.*"

Jack's nostrils flared as he finally caught up to the booth and came to a standstill before it, watching angrily as the Prickly Professor spread her legs wide open on a stage and the male announcer ran his fingers through her pussy hair, petting her like a kitty-cat. He knew it was all a rehearsed act, but goddamn he wanted to kill the son-of-a-bitch for touching her.

The men gathered around the stage started whistling and shouting while the male announcer petted her intimately, catcalls and loud boasts filling the air.

"*As much as our slutty little Krissy likes to get fucked,*" the announcer continued while his index finger rimmed the hole of her vagina, "*tonight she's in the mood to have her delicious cunt sucked on.*"

More whistling, louder catcalls and cheering. Krissy did as she'd been told to do, smiling down at the men in the audience while the announcer fondled her.

Jack gulped. It was the first time he'd ever seen her smile. Sweet Jesus he'd had no idea her cute little cheeks were dimpled. But goddamn it if that bastard didn't quit touching her...

"*Shall I suck on it first to find out how sweet her juice tastes?*"

Jack's jaw clenched hotly. If that motherfucker put his face anywhere near her pussy he was a dead man.

"*On second thought, it's the right of the lucky winner to get the first and only taste of this succulent cunt tonight, so gentlemen, let's start the contest. The winner,*" he finished as he tweaked one of her nipples, "*gets to play with this gorgeous slut's body while he drains her dry.*"

Jack pushed his way to the front of the line, willing to do whatever it took to be declared the winner. He didn't know yet what kind of a contest it was and he didn't care.

If Krissy was getting her pussy sucked on tonight, it would be by him.

* * * * *

Kris' heartbeat went into overdrive as she watched Jack's teeth grit and the veins on his massively muscled arm bulge. *Oh lord*, she thought as she bit on her lower lip, *don't lose now, Jack. You've made it to the final two for goodness sake.*

She knew he had to be tired. He was arm-wrestling his sixth and final opponent while she lay back on her elbows on the stage above the competitors, her legs spread wide at the knees, and watched. Occasionally she fondled herself as she'd been instructed to do, or glanced down into the arena of men to wink at them while she rubbed her nipples, but for the most part her gaze remained trained on Jack.

At first she hadn't known what to think when he'd beaten his first opponent. She'd spent the greater part of the day talking herself out of thinking about Jack, only to have him show up at the first contest she'd been placed as a prize in and try to win the right to perform oral sex on her.

Quite frankly she hadn't expected for this many men to be interested in winning the right to eat her out, so as it turned out Jack had his work cut out for him.

Not a bad showing for a woman with five cats, she sniffed.

Kris' heart rate sped up impossibly further as more and more men began circling Jack and Lauren, waiting to see who would emerge the victor. Lauren was big and muscular like Jack so it was hard to tell which one of the two would win.

She had to admit, she was getting pretty turned on watching Jack arm-wrestle for her. He looked sexy in the jeans that molded perfectly to his body and the sexy black shirt that showed off his muscular arms. And then there was the way his teeth were gritted and his muscles were corded and slick with perspiration...

Very hot.

Knowing he was doing it for the right to perform oral sex on her—extremely hot.

And yet, perversely, she was as afraid of Jack winning as she was afraid of Jack losing. Because if he won he would get to touch her for a full thirty minutes and she didn't know if she could handle it.

When all was said and done, after all, Kris would go back to being the boring professor of anthropology and Jack would go back to dating his dumb airheads. She wasn't certain she could stomach seeing him with a beautiful, built blonde on his arm after spending so much intimate time with him. Every moment that she spent with him would make their inevitable parting of company that much more difficult.

Or, at least, it would for her.

"He's almost got him pinned," one man jovially called out before sipping on his glass of champagne.

Kris' eyes widened as she tried to make out who had almost pinned whom. But so many men were gathered around now that she couldn't make out much of anything.

"Come on buddy, I've got three hundred bucks riding on you!" another man called out.

A couple of minutes later, when loud cheers went up like wildfire, Kris' heart damn near beat out of her chest. She could tell by the loud ruckus that a winner had been declared, but had no idea if that winner was Jack or Lauren.

She lay there in wait, her breasts dramatically heaving up and down, as she tried to calm her breathing.

And as she waited for the victor to emerge from the circle of men to orally perform on her.

Two sets of hands grabbed her from behind, lifting her up. She gasped.

"It's okay," one of the young men who worked at Hotel Atlantis said in low tones. "We're just carrying you to the pillows to make the next half hour more comfortable for you is all."

"But who won?" she breathed out as the young, muscular men carried her to the middle of the stage and laid her down within an enclave of lush pillows that resembled a harem bed. "Who won?" she asked again, wide-eyed.

"I'm not sure," the man who had announced her on stage admitted. "I couldn't see over the crowd. Still can't." He smiled at her. "It'll be okay, Kris. Just remember if you don't like the guy it only lasts for thirty minutes."

But thirty minutes with Jack McKenna could go a long way toward breaking her heart, she silently admitted. Not that she could tell the guys that. They'd all think she was nuts, not realizing her history with him.

Try to remember you're just a prostitute to him, Kris. No matter who walks out of the circle a winner, to both men you are nothing more than a prostitute.

And then she saw them. Both of them. Jack and Lauren shook hands as any good sportsmen would do after a winner had been declared, then broke away from each other. Her heart began thumping in overtime again as she stared wide-eyed at both of them, waiting to see which one would walk away and which one would climb the twig-like steps of the log stage...

She gasped as he took the stairs two at a time, his breathing ragged and his upper body soaked in perspiration.

"Jack," she whispered.

* * * * *

Jack ignored the congratulatory remarks and the whooping victory sounds being sent up on his behalf as he narrowed his dark gaze at the object of his lust and obsession. Like a charging bull in full rut, he headed straight toward the bed of pillows she was lying in.

"Jack," she whispered, her green eyes wide. "You won."

"Disappointed?" he asked a bit gruffly. He was pumped full of a dangerous mix of adrenaline, possessiveness, and testosterone—the three elements he'd used to his advantage tonight to insure his victory. "I told you not to let another man touch your pussy," he gritted out. "That announcer..."

"He's gay," she said quickly. "It was just an act."

Jack grunted, realizing that part of her statement wasn't true. He'd known the announcer for a few years and the man was definitely not gay. Still, he also realized that Krissy probably believed that statement to be true because it was a common lie the announcers often told to the new women to make them feel more comfortable with being fondled by them during the pre-contest shows.

He stared down at her, his emotions wild. He felt like an animal. He wanted to tell Krissy that she meant more to him than a prize at a contest, that he'd fought to win her just so no other man could touch what he already considered to be his, but all he could think about at the moment was that he was damn tired and she belonged to him and him alone for the next thirty minutes.

And sweet Jesus did she look good to him.

Lounging back on the pillows, her thighs spread wide apart, he stared at her exposed cunt, ready to devour it. It was ruby red and puffed up, telling him without verbal confirmation that she was already highly aroused.

He saw her breathing hitch as he came down on his knees before her, settling himself between her legs. Her breasts heaved up and down as she made eye contact with him, her nipples jutting up, seeking attention.

Jack palmed her breasts, then ran his hands up and down the length of her chest, watching her breathing grow increasingly labored while he did so. He ran his hands over her breasts as if spreading suntan oil on them, watching her body writhe from the friction against her nipples.

He glanced back down between her legs and felt his mouth begin to water. "I worked real hard for this pussy tonight, sweetheart," he growled. "So lay back and enjoy the next thirty minutes because my face will be buried between your legs the entire time."

He saw her wet her lips, whether out of nervousness or anticipation he couldn't say. And that was the last thing he saw before his face dove between her thighs and his mouth clamped onto her cunt like a baby to a pacifier.

"Jack," she breathed out, her back arching. "Oh god, Jack."

He heard her breathy moans somewhere in the back of his mind, but like a man possessed he could think only about the flesh he was sucking on. He growled low in his throat as he took her clit between his lips and began firmly suctioning it with his tongue.

She arched her back again, grinding her cunt against his face as she wrapped her legs around his neck and moaned. "*Yes,*" she groaned, her breathing labored. "*Oh Jack, yes.*"

He grunted arrogantly as she writhed beneath him, his mouth firmly latched around her clit. He sucked on the swollen piece of flesh hard, and harder still, growling incoherently against her pussy that her cunt belonged to him.

Jack ignored the whooping sounds the men continued to make as they voyeuristically watched him eat Krissy out. He even managed to ignore it when they gathered closer around the bed of pillows and made appreciatory comments about her body.

"I love her tits," he heard one say.

"Damn I want to fuck her," another one said thickly.

He managed to ignore them only because he knew none of them would ever get the chance to touch her. What belonged to Jack McKenna belonged only to Jack McKenna, and the pussy he was feverishly sucking on was definitely his.

He went in for the kill then, sucking her clit firmly and vigorously, growling low in his throat as she bucked up beneath him. On a loud groan she burst, her legs violently trembling as her nipples stabbed up and she drenched his mouth with her sweet climax.

He lapped it all up, gluttonously sucking at her hole to get every drop of liquid her cunt had made for him...

From somewhere in the haze of her mind, Kris heard the shouts and the cheers, heard the other men laughing lustily as they watched her aching nipples stiffen impossibly further and stab upward, but she was so aroused that all she could concentrate on was the face buried between her legs.

She moaned as he continued to lick her and lap at her, groaning when he started the process all over again, sucking on her pussy as if he couldn't get enough of it.

"Jack," she gasped as he latched his mouth around her clit again and began suckling it. "Oh god Jack I can't take anymore."

But he didn't stop. She thought he'd never stop. He licked at her and toyed with her, nibbled on her flesh and then sucked it like candy.

She came three more times before the thirty minutes was over. Three impossibly violent times during which each orgasm was stronger than the last.

By the time the thirty minutes had all but drawn to a close, at least fifteen men were surrounding the bed of pillows to watch. She heard the comments that were being made about her. She heard it all, but paid it little heed. By the time the announcer called the oral sex session over, by the time Jack raised his dark head from between her quivering thighs, she was aching and half-delirious, the violence of her orgasms leaving her as weak as an infant and breathing as raggedly as if she'd just run ten miles.

"Mine," Jack murmured, causing her to seek out his gaze. "This pussy is all mine, baby."

She closed her eyes, wondering what he meant by that. His tonight? His while she was on the island?

Or his forever?

She sighed, realizing how ridiculous her thoughts had become.

Chapter Nine

She didn't know what to think when Jack entered the second contest. Afraid to hope it meant something more than lust, she decided not to think about it at all and to simply enjoy the remainder of the night—and Jack's sexual awareness of her—at face value.

The second contest was pretty tame compared to the first one. Basically the men threw javelins and whoever threw theirs the furthest got to have a bunch of risqué photographs taken with the prize, the prize at this stage of the night being herself.

Truthfully, Kris was more hesitant about this contest than the first one. Not because she minded taking risqué photographs per se, but because she didn't want any of these men to leave the island with potential blackmail material to lord over her. She couldn't chance anyone at the university ever seeing photographs of her sprawled out all naked and oiled up on a clothed man's lap.

Quite frankly, she wasn't altogether certain what she would do when the fifteen-minute photo session arrived. For the life of her she couldn't figure out a graceful way to deny the winner of the contest his "winnings".

When she saw Jack enter the contest, her hope renewed. She was pretty sure the javelin competition would be won by either him or Lauren, and if it was Jack who won it she had a better chance of talking him out of taking the photographs with her than she did with Lauren.

Propped up on her elbow as she reclined on another one of those harem pillow kind of beds, Kris watched the javelin competition with keen interest. She bit her lip when it was

Jack's turn, and felt strangely proud of him when his javelin whizzed through the air and landed a yard further than the javelin of the man who had been in the lead.

"Why are you even in this competition?" she heard the displaced competitor grumble as he stalked off. "You just ate the slut's pussy out thirty minutes ago."

She tensed up when she saw Jack's nostrils flare, and worried for a long moment that he might do something rash to defend her honor. She could tell he didn't like the fact that the loser had called her a slut any more than she had liked it. The knowledge that Jack cared enough to become protective of her was heady indeed, but she didn't want him brawling and possibly hurting the guy either.

Kris' teeth sank into her lower lip as she watched Jack prowl toward the man. She blew out a breath of relief when the contest's announcer came between the two of them and calmed the situation down.

She watched for the next fifteen minutes as ten more competitors tried to outdistance Jack with their throwing arms. She could have sworn she'd seen his muscles tense up a couple of times when the javelins of two different competitors had come close enough to warrant a measuring stick being brought out and, again, had to wonder at it.

Stop reading more into his every gesture than is there, idiot! Just enjoy the night and his attention while it's still yours.

Lauren was the final competitor. Kris' heart raced as the handsome Frenchman's javelin went whizzing through the air, further and further, and —

Her eyes widened as she waited like the others for the measuring stick to be brought out. *Oh good lord,* she thought anxiously, her belly knotting, *I'll never be able to talk Lauren out of taking those photos. Please tell me Jack won!*

She swallowed roughly when the announcer said something that sent Jack into a rage. Her heart was beating so fast and so furiously that she could barely make out the words being angrily shouted back and forth between Jack and Lauren with the announcer trying to calmly intervene between the two men.

"There's no way this dick tied me!" Jack bellowed, his jaw hotly clenched. "No way in the hell!"

"Alor!" Lauren shouted back, his muscles clenching. "Zuh measure stick does not lie!"

"Zuh measure stick does not lie," Jack mimicked in a really bad French accent, his eyes rolling around comically. Kris stifled the urge to grin.

Jack slashed his hand through the air. "Hell yes it lied and I want a rematch!"

"Sir," the announcer said calmly. "You've both won. What's the big deal? Both of you get your prize so calm down."

"I do not," Jack said distinctly, his words precise, "share." His nostrils flared. "Ever."

Lauren folded his arms across his chest. One arrogant eyebrow rose mockingly. "Apparently tonight you do," he murmured.

Kris bit her lip when she saw Jack's jaw clench. He looked dangerous right now. Gloriously, arousingly dangerous.

When both men were led up to where she was lounging on the harem pillows she shifted her gaze hesitantly toward a very pissed off Jack. She thought back on last night when they'd mutually masturbated each other in the tiki bar and took a deep breath.

"Don't let another man touch your cunt," he warned her. "I mean it, Krissy. I couldn't handle it."

Hardly a Hallmark moment, but still quite heady.

Kris' head shot up at the sound of the announcer's voice. "You're going to take photos with Mr. Thibauld first," the announcer said under his breath to her. "Let's hurry up and get it over with so the grizzly bear doesn't cause any more trouble."

She expelled the breath she'd been holding in and nodded as she rose to her feet. "On the lounging chair?" she asked quietly, her heart racing. She was afraid she was about to give Lauren Thibauld blackmail material to hold over her, but even that worry paled in comparison to what she feared Jack might do as a result of this. He wouldn't physically harm her, she knew, but what if he refused to speak to her again?

And why should she care? Good lord the man was driving her insane! She didn't even recognize her own thought processes anymore, she thought grimly.

"Ah, there you are, ma chere," Lauren said on a grin as his eyes raked over her naked, oiled up body. "I would have rather won the last contest, but I will settle for what I can get. Tonight anyway."

Which meant he planned to bid on her tomorrow.

Would Jack bid on her too? she asked herself nervously, afraid to make eye contact with him. Or was all now lost?

As if it's your fault! As if Jack cares about you as a person any more than Lauren does!

She didn't know if her mental musings were the truth or not, only that she needed to bolster herself with such thoughts to get through the next fifteen minutes of photos with Lauren without grieving over what might be lost with Jack. And if Lauren planned to bid on her, well, it didn't hurt to have him see her in a positive light. After all, she'd be in his hut for three solid days if he won the auction, and more or less at his mercy for the remainder of the island excursion. The last thing she needed was for the Frenchman to be angry with her. But if she let Lauren touch her between the legs as he'd be expecting to do...

Good lord, what a dilemma.

You're the one who wanted to get a life, she grimly reminded herself. *Well congratulations because you've got one in spades!*

Lauren was dressed in costly, tailor made clothing, his cologne as expensive in scent as his attire. She hesitantly crawled up onto his lap, tensing momentarily when she felt his erection pressing against the confines of his tweed trousers. She forcibly relaxed and plastered a smile on her face.

Lauren's gaze drank in her nude body, his eyes heavy-lidded. "You have a beautiful smile, ma chere." He placed his hand on her thigh and began gently massaging it as his gaze dropped down to her chest. "And exquisite breasts," he murmured. "I cannot wait until zuh auction is over and you are mine."

She didn't need to look at Jack to know that the Frenchman's words, coupled with the fact it was inevitable Lauren would touch her intimately, had made his muscles tense up. She could sense his physical reaction even with her face turned away from him.

Lordy, lordy.

She cleared her throat, smiling at Lauren as he continued to stroke her thigh. She could hear the photographer snapping photos, ceaseless camera clicks making her all the more nervous.

Against her volition, she felt the beginnings of arousal stir in her belly and felt oddly guilty for it. But she was sitting naked on a clothed man's lap, she mentally excused herself, and the chill in the night air was making her nipples stand erect.

When the tip of Lauren's index finger gently grazed the peak of one of her stiff nipples and flicked it, she drew in a shaky breath. She could practically hear Jack's teeth gritting and wasn't certain what to do.

You're a prostitute to Lauren. And to Jack. Try to remember that, Kris.

"C'est vrai," Lauren whispered thickly. "I will play with your gorgeous nipples for three full days, ma chere."

Thankfully he didn't try to touch her breasts again, but then the fingers of one of his hands slowly began trailing down her belly, toward the place Jack had warned her about. "And," he said hoarsely, "I will fuck your cunt all day and night."

She panicked when she heard Jack mutter something belligerent. Her hand flew to cover Lauren's a fraction of a second before it would have dropped to her mons. "I'm a bit shy," she said in a nervous rush. Her breasts heaved when she took a deep breath. "Can't we wait until tomorrow, daddy?"

Kris watched his eyes narrow in desire and knew then and there that Elizabeth had been right about Lauren. He liked for prostitutes he bought to pretend they were little girls. If he successfully purchased her at the auction tomorrow, then according to Elizabeth, he'd make her shave her intimate hair and wear pigtails for the entire three days they spent together.

Lauren's eyelids were so heavy they almost looked closed. "Daddy will have to punish you tomorrow for making him wait," he murmured, his erection growing. "But you will like that, n'est pas?"

She wet her lips, wondering what he meant by punishment. Perhaps this game was more advanced than she'd bargained for. "Yes," she hesitantly replied, forcing a dimpled smile onto her face.

"Then we will wait," he said thickly. He cleared his throat. "Now then, turn around on daddy's lap and spread your legs wide apart for zuh camera. Bon. What a good girl you are, ma chere. Daddy will hold you while you stroke your pussy for zuh camera."

She could feel Jack tensing up impossibly further, though she still refused to look at him to visually confirm it. And yet as angry as he was, her sixth sense also told her that he was arrogantly pleased by the fact that she'd purposely found a way to keep Lauren from touching her intimately. With the exception of one slight graze to her nipple, he hadn't gone as far as either of them had thought he would.

Jack might not be happy with the fact that Lauren's arms had come around her from behind so his hands could massage her belly, the tips of his fingers occasionally finding the beginning of her dark red triangle, but he was satisfied that she'd thwarted the Frenchman from playing in her vagina or fondling her breasts any further than he already had.

Kris masturbated herself on Lauren's lap, his soft groans telling her he could see what she was doing by watching a television-like screen that showed what was happening from the front. She carefully kept her head averted the entire time, concealing her facial features from the forever-snapping camera.

When she finally came, she did so on a soft groan, her nipples stiffening as her head fell back on Lauren.

"Bon fille," he murmured in her ear. "Good girl."

She closed her eyes and sighed, relieved when the announcer told Lauren his fifteen minutes were up. She plastered a smile on her face as she rose up from his lap, still refusing to look at Jack.

Lauren inclined his head to her. His eyes raked over her nipples, over her cunt. "See you tomorrow, beautiful." And with that, he winked and strolled away.

Kris blew out a breath, relieved. But then moments later her body stiffened when she heard the announcer tell Jack he could take the seat Lauren had vacated.

Hesitantly, she lifted her gaze to Jack, watching as he slowly prowled toward her. He looked so sexy in his perfectly fitted denim jeans and black tee-shirt that the mere sight of him made butterflies swim in her belly.

He came to a standstill before her, his nostrils flaring and his jaw clenched as his dark gaze bore into hers. "I'm feeling mighty dangerous right now, sweetheart," he drawled.

She blew out a breath. "But I stopped him from—"

"I know," he gritted out in a voice that sounded surprisingly pained. "But he almost touched your—"

"But he didn't," she said quickly and placatingly. She sighed, at a loss for what to say. "What could I do, Jack? I..."

"Make it up to me," he gritted out. "Goddamn it, Krissy, logically I know the way I feel isn't your fault, but I still need you to make it up to me."

Her eyes flew up to meet his. She took a calming breath. "This is getting very complicated," she whispered. *And very confusing,* she mentally added.

"Make it up to me."

She stilled. "What do you want me to do?" she heard herself ask, if a bit hesitantly.

His nostrils flared as he plunked down into the lounger and pulled her onto his lap. "All those nasty pictures you wouldn't take with Frenchy?" he growled. "I want you to take them with me." His eyebrow rose in challenge. "And I want you to look at the camera and smile with those pretty dimples showin' while you do it," he murmured.

She flinched. He'd found her Achilles Heel, she thought nervously. She didn't want any blackmail material leaving the island. "But I..."

Jack grunted. He'd never show the pictures to anyone, only keep them for himself, but he wanted her to figure that out for herself. "Smile," he said thickly as he turned her around on his lap so her back was against his chest.

He opened his knees to spread her thighs apart, his hands immediately zeroing in on her vagina. He used both sets of calloused fingers to spread apart her labial lips, exposing her pussy fully to the camera. "Smile," he murmured, his erection poking against her buttocks.

Kris blew out a shaky breath. She felt so damn aroused both by his fingers touching her down there as well as from having been ordered to do something naughty by Jack. But she was also very afraid to give him this much power over her. If she did this thing for him then he would have photographic evidence of her trip to Hotel Atlantis…

Hesitantly, nervously, she looked straight into the camera and smiled, dimples popping out on either cheek. The photographer snapped what felt like a million pictures of Jack holding open her labial lips while she sat there on his lap and smiled, her thighs spread wide.

"Play with your nipples, baby," he said thickly, one of his hands continuing to hold apart her pussy lips while the fingers of his other hand began massaging her clit. "And keep smiling while I make you cum."

It felt like an impossible task. Especially when his intimate massage became firm, the pressure he exerted against her clit unbearably arousing. She began to squirm, her head falling back on a moan.

"Look at the camera."

She looked at the camera and smiled. Her breathing hitched when her hands found her breasts. She shuddered and groaned when her thumbs and index fingers began massaging her own nipples, stretching and pulling them, tweaking and rolling them around.

"Keep smiling," he instructed her, his voice arrogantly aroused. "Show everyone how badly you want to please me and only me, sweetheart."

By now several men had gathered around to watch, so they were obviously the everyone Jack was referring to. This exhibitionist activity had already been getting her increasingly turned on, but smiling at the men and boldly looking them in the eyes while Jack pleasured her made her feel like a compliant whore.

Exactly the sort of dirty, submissive gesture she often fantasized about.

Exactly the sort of dirty, submissive gesture that brought her to orgasm when masturbating.

And so there on Jack's lap, one of her deepest, darkest fantasies was brought to life. She looked the men brazenly in the eyes while Jack masturbated her, grinning at them while she tugged at her nipples and massaged them, winking at them when they cheered her on, wanting her to cum in front of them.

The camera kept clicking.

She no longer cared.

Two of Jack's fingers penetrated her, causing her to gasp.

"Ride him!" one of the men shouted out.

"Let's see those tits bounce," another one said, causing the other male onlookers to chuckle.

"This is the last time you'll ever put on a show for any man but me, sweetheart," Jack growled in her ear. "So enjoy it while you can."

She did.

Kris moaned as she rode up and down on Jack's two fingers, her breasts jiggling sexily, as the men shouted out praise and the camera photographed it all. She arched her back so the camera could get a better view of her penetrated cunt, her gaze trained on the male audience as she occasionally grinned at them between moans.

She rode Jack's fingers faster and faster, deeper and harder, then faster and faster still. She boldly made eye contact with each and every one of the men while she pumped up and down on Jack's fingers, her wet flesh making suctioning sounds on every upstroke.

She felt so wicked, so aroused, that she wanted to keep doing this all night. But eventually the need to orgasm became paramount and, with a loud groan, she threw her head back and climaxed violently all over Jack's hand.

Her nipples immediately stabbed out as blood rushed to heat her face and erogenous zones. She rode every wave of her orgasm out, frantically sheathing herself on Jack's fingers as his free hand reached around and tweaked at her stiff nipples.

Kris came down from the high slowly, a blissful look on her face as she unsheathed Jack's fingers from her vagina and turned around on his lap to face him. She wrapped her arms around his neck and threaded her hands through his hair. "Why don't you fuck me for real?" she whispered in an aroused voice, surprising him. "I've fantasized about you for years and—"

She gasped when two sets of strong arms plucked her out of his lap and handed her over to a third man.

"Fifteen minutes is up," the announcer threw over his shoulder to Jack, uncaring of the fact that Jack looked ready to kill him with his bare hands. "It's time for the next contest."

* * * * *

When Jack entered the third and final contest she was placed as a prize in, she was pretty certain she at last understood how he had felt during the other two competitions. This contest was called Poker King, and in this poker playing contest the winner took all.

Inevitably, the winner was Jack. Not that Kris was surprised by that singular fact. She was beginning to think that there wasn't a damn thing the surly man hadn't already mastered.

Either that or he wanted her to himself badly enough to master them quickly. She wanted to believe that was the case but…

Kris' nostrils flared when the male announcer threw a wrench into the works, adding a "bonus" into the contest that she hadn't been expecting.

"*This year's poker king will get an extra special treat,*" the announcer grinned as he guided a busty, naked blonde toward Kris. "*Your Majesty,*" he said loudly to Jack into the microphone he held in his hand, "*sit back in your throne and enjoy the view because these two gorgeous sluts are going to oil wrestle for the right to suck your cock.*"

Drunken cheers went up like wildfire, the male onlookers settling in to enjoy the show Kris hadn't even known would take place. She saw Jack lift an eyebrow as he looked at her, letting her know he wasn't at all sad to see this turn in events. The look he was giving her seemed to say *now you know how I've felt all goddamn night, sweetheart.*

Her nostrils flared as an irrational jealousy overwhelmed her. She had no claims to Jack and probably never would, but damn it if she'd sit back and watch another woman suck the Grinch off—

Kris gasped when the busty blonde grabbed her by the back of her hair and tried to shove her face into the dirt. A lusty roar of approval went up from the crowd, the men enjoying the view of two naked women wrestling over the "honor" of giving a blowjob.

Oh good lord, she thought, breathing heavily as she managed to squirm her way out of the woman's hold on her. *I'm an esteemed anthropologist for goodness sake! I will not, repeat NOT, wrestle a naked woman for the right to suck that man off!*

Her jaw clenched and her heart raced when the busty, naked beauty strolled over to Jack with a seductive smile on her face and leaned over to squeeze his cock through his trousers. "Yummy," she said, arching her back so her breasts were popping out before his face. "It's so big…"

That. Did. It.

"Hi-yeeeeeee!"

Kris screamed out her war cry at the same moment she jumped on the woman from behind, bringing her down to the ground. Cheers and roars of approval erupted from the crowd, some of the men standing up and whooping loudly while two naked, oil-slicked women rolled around on the grass trying to pin each other to it.

In her peripheral vision she could see Jack grinning, which made her all the madder. "I'm an anthropologist," she hissed to her competitor as she struggled with the woman.

"Yeah?" her competitor said belligerently. "So?"

"So I've lived with the Kung people of Africa, baby!" she ground out as she rolled the woman onto her back and tried to straddle her. "And war-mongering native tribes in the Rainforest." She sniffed, hoping she looked like an authority on the subject. "Nobody but nobody can wrestle like those guys."

Her competitor grunted, but said nothing as they rolled.

More cheers, louder shouting.

"And I once dated a guy who was the friend of a friend who did time in Attica!"

Her competitor snorted as she grabbed her by the back of the head and tried to shove her face into the dirt again. "So what! What does that have to do with anything?" she sneered.

Nothing, but it had sounded intimidating to Kris at the time and she had hoped the same effect would happen on Betty Big Boobs. Apparently not, she grimaced, when the woman offered her a stinging backhand across the face.

"Did I mention the fact that—"

"Bah! Just shut up and wrestle me, bitch!"

Bitch, she thought angrily, her adrenaline surging. The bitch had dared to call her a bitch!

"Hi-yeeeeee!"

Kris screamed out her war cry for a final time when, in a show of great strength, she threw her competitor to the ground, quickly straddled her lap, and pinned both of her arms to the ground.

"One," the announcer bellowed into the microphone as the men in the crowd roared. Her competitor wriggled madly beneath her. *"Two...three. Winner!"*

Kris could scarcely believe it, but she'd actually won. She grunted as she drew herself up to her knees, feeling oddly proud of her accomplishment.

She felt like an Olympic gold medallist. She felt like the heavyweight boxing champion of the world.

She felt like a moron, she thought grimly.

And when she heard Jack's loud, booming laughter, she felt like a ninny to boot.

How funny he must think it is, she thought with a sense of hurt pride, to see the boring Professor Torrence reduced to this. She had only wanted to have one wild experience to treasure in her memories, not humiliating ones like this.

She covered her ears when the cheering grew louder, embarrassment crashing over her until her cheeks went up in flames and tears filled her eyes.

She could see Jack laughing, the sight of which made the tears want to spill down her cheeks. She could well imagine what her nemesis thought of seeing her reduced to this.

Panicked, hurt, and a million other things, Kris bolted from the contest arena with her hands still clapped over her ears, the sound of male laughter and cheering humiliating to her.

"I want to go home," she choked out as she ran. "I just want to go home."

Jack watched her run away, his smile fading as her crying form disappeared into the dark night. He sighed, feeling guilty that he hadn't kidnapped his little witch away from this place the moment he'd clapped eyes on her. He had figured the island would eventually get to her and wasn't the least bit surprised when the auspicious moment finally arrived.

That's what you get for trying to play by the rules in a mad land, idiot, he chastised himself.

He sighed as he walked away, waving off the wrestling match's loser when she came toward him trying to offer a consolation prize.

He didn't want any other woman. Only Krissy.

From now on he'd never pay attention to anybody else's rules again.

Chapter Ten

By the time Kris fell limp into her bed that night, her muscles were achingly sore and her head hurt from all the crying she'd gone off and done in private.

She had searched for John and Sheri for over an hour, wanting to retrieve her clothing and take a chartered flight out of here. But they were nowhere to be found and she feared she was going to end up having to go through with the auction tomorrow night whether she wanted to or not.

And she definitely didn't want to.

For the first time since she'd arrived on Atlantis Island, Kris didn't want to be bought by any man at the sex slave auction tomorrow night. If Jack was outbid, she feared she wouldn't have as good of a time with whatever man won—probably Lauren?—as she would if she spent the remaining three days catering to Jack's sexual whims.

Scratch that. She *knew* she wouldn't have as good of a time. Jack had been the sole focus of her submission fantasies for the past two solid calendar years.

On the other hand, if Jack won the auction and successfully purchased her for the remaining three days then that opened an entirely new Pandora's Box. She was terribly embarrassed about tonight's events and wasn't certain she could handle looking him in the eye after having humiliated herself by wrestling in the nude with another woman for the right to give him oral sex. Then humiliated herself all over again by running off crying the way she had.

Kris closed her eyes tightly, the embarrassment swamping her senses all over again. Good lord, what Jack must think of her...

What was she to Jack anyway? she wondered for the hundredth time tonight. A contest prize, a pathetic spinster he wanted to mount, or something more?

She sighed, hugging the soft covers to her body as she slowly drifted off to sleep.

*****

Jack let himself into John's private hut, a lush paradise on the far side of the island, filled with exotic plants, expensive tropical looking furniture, and when he felt like it, exotic naked women. Today John felt like it.

When Jack let himself in through the living room window, he followed the sound of John's moans and murmurs down the long, twisting hallway and into the den. The den had always been John's favorite getaway, a personal retreat that was the only part of the house that Jack could tell had been decorated by his longtime buddy's own hand. The rest of the hut was classy and tropical-looking but it just didn't say John. It said man-with-many-old-wounds-trying-to-pretend-he's-someone-he's-not.

Namely, a rich, arrogant asshole.

The rich part was true. The rest of it wasn't.

Jack was surprised when he rounded the corner and entered the den to find John inside with three naked women. The sight immediately sent warning bells off in his head because for as long as John had owned the island he'd never once allowed a woman, let alone three prostitutes, to enter his private lair.

Any other room in the hut and Jack wouldn't have thought anything of it. But a foursome in John's personal getaway? Big-time warning bells.

Sweet Jesus. Sheri was right. Something was very wrong.

"*Talk to him, Jack,*" Sheri had pleaded with him when she'd come to his hut a few minutes before fleeing the island for reasons she wouldn't name. "*I don't know what the hell is going on, but he's worrying me. John trusts and respects you. He'll talk to you. But me...?"* She'd shaken her head and sighed. *"I'll always be the kid sister in his eyes. John thinks he's supposed to know more than I do. He'll never listen to me."*

When Jack drew closer to the foursome, the strong scent of bourbon and marijuana choked the air, sending off the most frightening warning bells yet. *John's never been much of a drinker,* he thought. *Or a smoker.*

Naked, John was lying down on a huge two-seater chair that reclined into a bed. One leg bent at the knee, his arms relaxed behind his head, his eyes were closed while he moaned, three naked women kissing and sucking his various body parts.

Jack immediately recognized the woman sucking him off as Cherice, a Los Angeles madam originally from Paris who worked two island excursions a year as a prostitute because of the high pay involved. John and Cherice had become good friends over the years, but rarely did the two become sexual. And it definitely wasn't like Cherice, a businesswoman through and through, to waste valuable time flirting with tonight's potential buyers in order to suck off John for free.

Screaming, screeching, neon lights flashing kind of warning bells.

Something was definitely wrong with John Calder if even Cherice LeMont recognized it. Was she here to comfort him? Or, he thought worriedly, to watch him? Damn it, why was she worried enough to even be here?

And then he saw ebony hands running over John's chest, a beautiful ebony face bent to kiss him. Tanisha Jones. A Detroit madam who worked one island excursion a year as a prostitute for the high pay. Another good friend of John's wasting valuable flirting time to be with her employer for free.

What the hell?

Jack recognized the third woman as Krissy's friend Elizabeth, but had no idea how she fit into the picture. Of course it was also pretty well known that she and Tanisha were friends and that the third grade school teacher occasionally "entertained" clients of the madam's who were visiting the San Diego area. So maybe the Detroit madam had asked Elizabeth to come here tonight.

But, again, why? What the hell was going on?

John's head fell back into Tanisha's lap on a groan, his muscles cording and tensing as he spurted into Cherice's mouth. His breathing was heavy, his body soaked with perspiration, as he came down from the orgasmic high and slowly fell into a lulling, if drunken sleep.

Tanisha continued to rub his chest, Elizabeth his legs and belly, and Cherice sang—a French lullaby to him? *What!*—until all three of them were certain he was sound asleep. Only then did they get up.

"Well," Cherice whispered in a thick accent as she stood up, "he should be asleep until zuh morning. Let us go, eh?"

Tanisha nodded, then threw five strands of long microbraids over her shoulder. "I stole his gun so that's not a worry. Not tonight anyway. And Lizzy did away with the pills. So those are outta the picture until he gets refills on the mainland."

Jack's jaw went slack. Gun? Pills? Sweet Jesus, did they think he was gonna—

"Jack!" Cherice urgently whispered as she walked toward him, her naked body glistening with coconut oil. "Keep an eye on our old friend, eh? We have to go to work, cher."

Jack absently nodded as his gaze flew back to John. "What the hell is wrong with him?" he murmured. "Why are you three here?"

Cherice sighed as she patted him on the shoulder. "His mind is, uh..." She stumbled over her English, looking for the proper words.

"Fucked up," Tanisha provided for her with a frown.

Cherice nodded. "As to why—alor, we do not know, cher."

Jack nodded. "Thanks for, uh…" He cleared his throat and glanced away. "Taking care of him," he finished dumbly.

Tanisha chuckled at that. "No problem. But Cherice is right. We gotta get back to work. Look after him, okay?"

"Yeah," Jack said distractedly as they strolled out of the hut, his mind working out the situation and coming up with no answers. "Keep the gun," he said absently as he walked toward John.

Tanisha harrumphed. He could hear her talking to the others as they left the hut together. "If that ugly-ass Russian guy bids on me I'll probably use it too…"

Once the women had left, Jack turned his full attention back to his friend John.

John, who was sprawled out drunk and asleep on the recliner, snoring loudly. John, who from all accounts was acting crazy enough lately that everyone was worried he was going to do something dangerous to himself.

Johnny, his best friend since age eight.

Jack sat there for over a half hour, absently watching John sleep as he tried to pinpoint where it had all gone wrong. It couldn't have been his childhood like Sheri thought—those demons had been exorcized long ago. So what then? What had thrown him over the proverbial edge?

Five minutes later Jack sighed when John woke up groaning and, clutching his stomach, ran into the nearest bathroom as fast as his stumbling legs could move. He heard the lid to the toilet bowl clink against the back of the commode when it was flung up, then heard the sound of John retching his guts out, expensive bourbon and God knows what else spewing into the toilet.

Another five minutes passed before the retching and dry-heaving ceased. The sound of running water filled the hut next as John apparently showered himself clean.

When his best friend finally emerged ten minutes later wearing a pair of cotton drawstring pajama bottoms, he was clean but otherwise looked like hell. He had dark circles under his eyes as if he hadn't been sleeping and the usual lighthearted smile he wore was absent.

He watched as John sat down on a chair with a sigh, by now very aware of the fact he had company. The two men sat there in silence together for a long moment, neither speaking nor looking at each other. But finally Jack broke the silence.

"You gonna tell me about it, buddy?"

John softly snorted as he glanced at him. "What's to tell? My life sucks. Lots of people's lives suck."

Jack grunted. "Cherice and Tanisha seem to think yours sucks enough that you might try to kill yourself." He narrowed his eyes at John as he finally looked at him. "Even your sister thinks that. So what's the deal?"

John looked surprised, which made Jack release a pent-up breath. Obviously suicide had never crossed his mind, so at least that wasn't something he'd have to worry about.

"Sheri really thinks that?" John rasped out, his voice scratchy from liquor and marijuana. "Shit, I'm not that bad," he muttered as he ran a hand over his jaw.

"Then what is it, man? What the hell is wrong with you?" The question was asked in his usual gruff voice, but his eyes were clearly troubled.

John blew out a breath. "I don't think I can pinpoint it to any one thing." He shrugged, standing up to pour himself a glass of ice water across the room. "People rarely have one earth-shattering thing happen to them that sends them over the edge, buddy. Or at least I don't." He sighed. "It's just a culmination of lots of little things. I guess it's all finally getting to me," he muttered as he tipped the glass of ice water to his lips.

Jack's eyebrows shot up. "The island, you mean?"

John chugged down the ice water in three huge gulps, then set the glass down with a sigh. "Basically." He turned his head to look at Jack. "Remember the first time you came here, how you had a really great time?"

"Because it was all so new." He grinned. "Yeah, I had a great time the first time."

"And after that?" John asked softly.

Jack nodded. "Too weird. I don't like paying for sex and I don't want a venereal disease. And most of the men who frequent this place are strange as hell," he muttered.

"And you only come here once a year at best." John took a deep breath and blew it out. "Now imagine living here."

Jack grunted. He was quiet for a moment, then inclined his head. "Point taken," he grumbled.

John plunked back down in his chair and leaned forward, his elbows on his knees as he steepled his fingertips together. "I'm tired of only being with women I pay for," he admitted, his voice still scratchy. "And the ones I don't pay for are still with me because of the money."

Jack didn't say anything, just sat there and listened so he could get it out of his system.

He sighed. "I'm tired of the sex business. I'm tired of feeling like I'm not doing anything worthwhile with my life. I wanted to be rich." He shrugged. "Okay fine, so now I'm rich. But now that I am I don't want to do this anymore."

"So don't," Jack said simply.

John stood up with a growl. "Easier said than done. If I don't do this, then what?" He walked to the window and stared out of it. "I have to do *something*, Jack. I'm not a bum who can just laze around and do nothing. But this..." He shook his head. "The thrill ended years ago," he murmured.

Jack stood up with a sigh and patted him on the back. He'd never been much good with words and was even less skilled at expressing emotions, so he said the only thing that came to mind. "You gotta know when to hold 'em. You gotta know when to fold 'em. You gotta know when to walk away. You gotta—"

John turned his head and stared at him surrealistically.

Jack grunted. "What?"

"'The Gambler'," he said dryly. "I'm depressed as hell and the best you can come up with in the way of comfort is quoting Kenny Rogers." He shook his head. "Shit I hope I'm not that bad," he mumbled. "If I am, it sure as hell explains why women prefer to go to other women for comfort."

He grunted again. "My point, bud, is this: if you're not happy, then fuck this place. You've got plenty of money and you don't need to put up with any of this bullshit. You can do whatever you want to do. You can be all that you can be—"

John frowned. "Now you sound like a goddamn ad for the Army." He snorted, the twinkle back in his eyes. "Nevertheless, that was a simple but true statement."

Jack grunted. "I'm a simple but true man." He glanced at his watch. "Shit! I've got to get over to that auction. But listen, after I go get my woman I'll come back to check on you and we'll talk some more."

John's eyebrows rose. "Your woman?"

Jack sighed, his hand tiredly running over his jaw. "Remember the elusive witch I told you about that night when, kinda like you are now, I was sitting around drunk and depressed?"

"Yeah. So?"

He frowned. "Krissy and the witch are the same woman. Seems my prudish little professor decided she wanted to be a wild child for five days," he growled.

John chuckled. "I wasn't one hundred percent certain who she was, but I knew she wasn't doing it for the money." He wiggled his eyebrows. "So maybe this place had its use after all." His smile faded. "Though I'm still ready to close it down after this excursion."

"Don't blame ya, bud." Jack affectionately slapped him on the back. He sighed, changing the subject. "I don't like leaving you like this, Johnny."

John waved that away. "You've got a Frenchman to outbid. And really, Jack, I'm fine. I feel a hell of a lot better now that I've admitted how I feel to myself. And to you."

Jack nodded. "I'll still be back." He thought about the auction for a moment and frowned. "And if Frenchy outbids me, I'll be back with Krissy."

John snorted at that. "Plans for kidnapping her already?"

"Hell yeah," he growled. "I don't share." He frowned. "I don't want another man near her, okay?"

Which was Jack's way of saying he was falling fast and furiously for her. If he hadn't already.

John nodded. "Understood, bro."

"Good." He slapped him on the back again before turning on his heel to walk away. He stopped abruptly, a thought occurring to him, as he turned his head to face John. "Do you, uh..."

John's brow wrinkled when he didn't continue.

Jack cleared his throat and blushed. "Do you, you know..." He coughed into his hand. "You don't need a goddamn hug or something, do you?" he muttered.

John's blue eyes widened. He threw his head back and laughed.

"It ain't that funny."

When his best friend finally stopped laughing, Jack was happy to note that the twinkle hadn't disappeared from his eyes. "Um...no." John grinned. "But thanks for the offer."

Jack grunted. "Thank God. I would have, ya know, but it would have been weird." He frowned. "And I don't believe Kenny Rogers has a song about shit like that."

Chapter Eleven

On the night of the auction, Kris' nerves were wound as tight as a coiled spring. Forty women in total had been lined up, all of them wearing black silk robes that were draped in such a way as to show off their cleavage, and matching black silk thongs that were concealed by the thigh-length robes.

She thought it seemed a bit odd that, on all of the nights to clothe the women, John had elected to do so on the evening they were to be auctioned off to their three-day masters. But she supposed she could understand the psychology behind it, giving the high bidders the right to peel off the clothing of their sex slaves whenever and wherever they felt like doing it.

Strange, but she felt more naked while clothed than she'd felt while actually naked.

Because now she felt like a dressed up sex doll waiting in the store window to be purchased. And damn if the feeling didn't arouse her just as she'd known it would.

She would have to use that arousal to her advantage while wearing pigtails and a shaved mons for Lauren because she'd given up all hope of Jack attending the auction tonight when he'd failed to appear ten minutes ago as the opening bids had begun. Not that she wanted to face him again. Indeed, she had tried for the last several hours prior to the auction to find John Calder and beg her way back to San Francisco without being auctioned off at all. She hadn't been successful. Where John had gone off to she had no idea.

"Come on, boys," the auctioneer said as he opened Barbi's robe and, standing behind the woman, began fondling her large breasts and playing leisurely with her nipples. "Three days with these huge tits are worth a hell of a lot more than two thousand dollars. Do I hear twenty-five hundred?"

"Twenty-five hundred."

Barbi purred as the auctioneer began massaging her nipples from the base, stroking upward from areolas to tips over and over again.

"Do I hear three thousand?"

"Three thousand."

"Do I hear thirty-five hundred? Going once. Going twice. Sold to Mr. Lawrence for three thousand dollars."

Barbi smiled seductively at Mr. Lawrence. But then she would if she wanted to earn a big tip when the three days were over. She left the stage to join the other two women he'd already bought and paid for, both of them already on their knees taking turns sucking his cock while he leisurely sipped from a beer and watched the auction.

When Kris' name was called to come out on stage, she felt panicked enough to vomit. She took a steadying breath, told herself it would only be for three days, reminded herself that she really wanted to experience sexual submission to a man once in her life, and walked toward the stage with a welcoming smile on her face. Besides, John Calder had up and vanished so she had no way to escape the auction.

Cheers and catcalls immediately filled the room. The auctioneer wasted no time in taking advantage of that fact.

"The next slave up for purchase is Krissy, the island's only natural redhead, and one of the more popular girls during this excursion." He covered the microphone for a brief moment and muttered under his breath to her. "Calm down—I can see how nervous you are. Do this just like we practiced and you'll have a good time and all of us will walk out of here with bucket loads of money."

She nodded, and then smiled out to the cheering crowd.

Kris tensed up when she saw Lauren wink at her, wondering again what he had meant last night when he'd told her he meant to punish her for making him wait to fondle her. But when she considered the fact that she'd be at his mercy for the next three days, she decided to sweetly smile at him rather than stand there and worry.

He smiled back as he absently stroked the hair of the naked woman sitting at his feet. Like Mr. Lawrence, he had already purchased two other women, so she would be his third sex slave.

"We're starting the bidding on Krissy at three thousand dollars. Who will bid three thousand dollars to have the exclusive use of her succulent cunt for three nights in a row?"

She blew out a breath. This was so overwhelming.

"*I will.*"

Kris gasped at the sound of Jack's growling, surly voice. Her heart raced as she watched him stroll into the auction room wearing an expensive Italian business suit and a lot of attitude. But then he always wore those things.

She didn't know what to think or how to feel. Part of her was elated that he'd shown up, but the other part of her was embarrassed to see him again after the way she'd freaked out and ran off last night. Especially considering the fact he hadn't come after her.

Lauren's eyes narrowed at Jack. "Four thousand."

"Five thousand," Jack countered, not missing a beat.

Kris' eyes widened. *Why is Jack doing this?* she wondered, her heart wrenching more than she cared to admit. He hadn't followed her to the communal hut last night when she'd run off, so naturally when she'd had time to calm down and think things over she had assumed he wasn't interested in her anymore.

She blew out a breath. Perhaps her worst fear was true. Perhaps his interest in her didn't extend beyond the sexual. He was here tonight to bid on her for sexual purposes, but last night when she'd needed comfort he hadn't given her any, or even sought her out to make sure she was okay.

Or perhaps Jack had wanted to give you some time to be alone, believing you'd want to recuperate in your own way, an inner voice nagged.

Lauren scowled at Jack. "Six."

"Seven."

Kris gulped. She stared open-mouthed at the men, her gaze flicking back and forth from one to the other, for the life of her unable to understand why they'd spend so much money on a singular woman, and on herself in particular. Nevertheless, she thought as her heartbeat accelerated, this entire situation made one thing gloriously clear:

Jack wanted her. Even if only for three nights.

Even if only for sex.

And she did want to have sex with him—lots and lots of submissive sex.

It was time to let tomorrow take care of itself, she decided. For tonight she would revel in the knowledge that Jack was willing to spend seven thousand or more dollars to have sex with her for three days. When her time on the island was over she'd worry about her heart.

"Do I hear eight thousand dollars?" the auctioneer asked, looking pointedly at Lauren Thibauld.

The Frenchman's nostrils flared as he glanced at Jack. "Eight," he gritted out.

"Nine," Jack countered, cool as ice.

Silence.

"Mr. Thibauld?" the auctioneer inquired.

Lauren was quiet for a suspended moment. Kris was certain the entire room could hear the mad beating of her heart while they all awaited his answer. In fact, her heart was pumping so wildly she scarcely heard it when the auctioneer cried out, "Sold to Mr. McKenna for nine thousand dollars!"

She stood there dumbly, her legs feeling weak and her heart racing. The entire scene felt so surrealistic she couldn't seem to move.

"Go to Mr. McKenna," the auctioneer said under his breath to her. "He's waiting for you."

Kris' head came up slowly, her wide green eyes finding Jack's dark gaze. He crooked an arrogant finger at her and motioned with it for her to come to him.

She took a deep breath and, forgetting her earlier promise to herself, wondered again how she'd ever get through the next three days with her heart intact. She also wondered how she'd ever be able to face him on the mainland as if nothing had happened between them, as if she hadn't spent three days as his sex slave.

Lord help her, she was already in love with him.

Chapter Twelve

Kris quietly stood next to Jack as he paid the auction bill at a table that had been set up near the room's exit. His right hand was underneath the black silk robe she wore, absently caressing her buttocks as he waited for the cashier to process the payment to his credit card. She shivered when his finger lightly traced the cleft at the top of her buttocks, the spot extremely sensitive to touch.

"Thank you, Mr. McKenna," the cashier said as he handed the credit card back to him. "You're free to go."

Jack nodded, but said nothing. He patted Kris' backside to get her to move, but didn't speak to her as the two of them made their way to his hut. His calloused hand continued to stroke her bottom as they walked, that being the only communication there was between them.

Kris found the lack of words coupled with the light grazing of her buttocks extremely arousing. But she also found the silence deafening. She wondered to herself if Jack was angry that he'd forked nine thousand dollars over to spend three nights with her—wondered too if he was already regretting it.

Hey, it was his choice! she mentally sniffed. *If he's regretting it then he has nobody to blame but himself!*

Her chin thrust up as they continued to walk toward the hut—a defensive action that didn't go unnoticed by Jack. One of his eyebrows inched up as he glanced down at her, but he said nothing since she pretended not to notice him.

Only when they were at last inside of the hut, the thatched twig and stone doors closed firmly behind them, did Jack speak to her. "You better get off your high horse, professor," he said broodingly, unknotting his tie as he strolled toward the bureau. "Nine thousand dollars is a hell of a lot of money," he growled. "And I plan to get my money's worth."

Her chin remained notched. "I am not on my high horse," she said in a prim tone that for some reason or another Jack brought out in her as could no other. "However," she said regally, "I did not ask you to buy me." *I just hoped you'd want to.* "And," she finished quietly, glancing away, "I refuse to take the blame if you're not happy with the fact that you did."

His eyebrows rose as he took off his cufflinks and set them on top of the knotted pine bureau. He grunted. "Take off your robe. And, by the way, professor, who says I'm not happy?"

She hesitantly looked back at him. "You just seem sort of, I don't know." She waved a hand. "Surlier than normal I guess."

He rolled his eyes and sighed.

Her back went ramrod straight. "You don't need to make fun of me," she said in the pompous, prim tone she reserved for her arguments with Jack. She removed the robe as he'd barked at her to do, letting it flutter to the ground. "I was just trying to gauge your mood—"

"Krissy," he growled.

Jack closed his eyes when her chin inched up. He pinched the bridge of his nose for a long moment, sighing as his gaze flicked back to hers.

"Let me clue you in on something, sweetheart," he rumbled out, his eyes occasionally straying down to look at her naked breasts. "I paid nine *thousand* dollars to fuck the shit out of you. Nine *thousand* dollars." He frowned. "Maybe the weird rich guys who frequent places like this would spend nine thousand dollars on a woman *just because.* I don't."

Her pulse began to race. It wasn't exactly a proclamation of undying love, but it was a start. Her chin slowly anchored down to its normal position as she listened to the rest of his diatribe.

"I mean, no pussy is worth nine thousand dollars..."

She frowned at him as she felt her pulse return to normal. So much for making her heart quicken.

He grunted as he reached down beside the bed and picked up what looked to be her valise. "Except maybe yours," he conceded on a grumble.

Lordy, lordy—there went her damn pulse again. She wet her lips as she watched him slowly stroll toward her.

Jack's dark gaze raked over her naked breasts as he came to stand before her. She took a deep breath, her heartbeat working overtime. "Here," he barked as he handed her the valise.

Kris blinked. Her brow wrinkled as she hesitantly accepted the small suitcase from him. "I-I don't understand..." She felt like she was going to be ill. "You want me to get dressed and go home?" she breathed out.

His eyebrows drew together. "Hell no," he snapped, sounding every inch the surly beast she'd fallen head over heels for. "I want you to get dressed, but there's no way in the hell you're going home."

She sighed, one hand straying up to rub at her temples. "I don't understand..."

Jack pressed his big body in close to hers. He took one of her hands and placed it firmly over his erection. "Does this feel like I want you to leave?" he asked thickly.

Her heart began thumping heavily against her chest. "No," she whispered. It felt long and thick and hot—and hard as steel.

He ground his hips against her, grinding his cock into her palm. "I'm going to fuck you until you can't walk," he murmured. "I'm going to shoot so many loads of cum in your pussy in the next three days that you'll start to feel unnatural when you're not dripping my juices from between your legs..."

Her eyes widened as she stared at him, her arousal causing even her skin to tingle.

He placed his hand over hers and squeezed, smashing her palm harder against his erection. "But I want my professor," he rumbled out, his dark gaze raking over her face. "I want the real Kris Torrence, not the woman she's pretending to be for five days."

And suddenly she understood why he wanted her to get dressed, why he wanted her to put back on her drab university clothing...

Because he wanted to sexually dominate Kris, not Krissy. Because he was more interested in having sex with the professor than with the five-day prostitute.

She wet her lips as Jack released her hand, feeling nervous and unbelievably aroused. Jack wanted *her*—the real her. The unfashionable, average-looking, Dr. Kris Torrence. Any other man would have wanted the sex kitten. But Jack wanted the mouse.

Damn it, he was getting to her heart. He was no poet, that was for certain, but this gesture—and obviously one he'd taken the time to think on if he'd acquired her valise—was the biggest bolster to her sense of sexual self-worth she'd ever been given. She didn't have to pretend with Jack. She could just be herself.

Kris glanced away, nibbling at her lower lip. Lord this was confusing. On one hand she was elated by what he wanted her to do, but on the other hand she was terrified. She and Jack had a long history together, and other than what she now realized to have been tremors of sexual and emotional awareness that had passed between them, none of it had been pretty. They had squared off as if in battle for two years, yet now...

"You've had fantasies about me before then?" she whispered before resuming her nibbling.

Jack frowned. "For a Ph.D. you're not a very quick study." When she shot him a scathing look, he grunted in typical Jack fashion. "Lady, you have been my every dream and my every fantasy for the last two goddamn years..."

Her heart raced. Had she said he wasn't a poet?

"You've also been my every nightmare, but that's beside the point."

Her lips pinched together. Nope, definitely not a poet.

Jack slashed a hand through the air. "I just spent nine thousand dollars to get three days of on-demand submissive sex from you. I'll be damned if I'm not getting the professor for those three days." He flicked at one of her nipples with a finger as if he couldn't seem to help himself, then frowned as he strolled away. "I'll be back in an hour with food. Be dressed when I return so I can undress you."

Kris took a deep breath as she watched him stroll toward the doors, not knowing how to feel.

He raised an eyebrow as he looked at her from over his shoulder, his mouth unsmiling as always. "You're my possession," he murmured. "For the next three days, I own you."

Jack waited for her to nod her understanding. He left as soon as she did.

Chapter Thirteen
ಸಾ

His plan had been to wine her and dine her, to eat a leisurely meal with the woman he'd never thought to be out on a real date with and just stare at her for a while, knowing she was there and wasn't leaving—and knowing he could do whatever he wanted to do to her whenever he wanted to do it. After that he had planned to seduce her, to spend a few minutes laying down the ground rules for the next three days so she'd know exactly how kinky he was and could tell him honestly whether or not she could handle it.

His good intentions flew out the proverbial window the second he walked through the doors and saw her. She was sitting on the bed with her hands on her lap, her hair pulled back into its deathly tight bun, those ugly as sin black spectacles perched on the tip of her nose, and was wearing the drabbest, most godforsaken unfashionable blue skirt and prim cotton shirt he'd ever had the displeasure of seeing.

Goddamn, he wanted her so bad he almost came in his trousers.

Jack's eyes flicked over to the far side of the room where black handcuffs dangled from the ceiling. His gaze narrowed in arousal as he slowly walked toward her. "Stand up," he said thickly. "Now."

She bit her lip. It was then that he realized how much of a difference the professor clothes made for her too. She didn't see this as a game any more than he did now. Suddenly it was very real to her that Dr. Kris Torrence was about to get fucked long and hard by Jack McKenna—a man who for all intents and purposes had been her nemesis for two solid years.

"Only when we have sex, Krissy," he rumbled out. "I only want and expect your submission when we have sex."

She hesitated for a moment, but in the end she stood up.

"Good girl," he murmured as he reached for her spectacles and absently tossed them into a nearby chair. He took her hand and led her to the far side of the hut. When they were there, he turned her around to face him.

She looked scared—real scared. Without a doubt, the reality of the situation had at last dawned on her.

Was she regretting the fact that the man she'd spent two years of her life going toe-to-toe with had purchased her and now held the upper hand? Jack wondered. He felt sick at his stomach when it occurred to him that she might be wishing she was with the Frenchman right now, or with any man but himself.

His jaw clenched. He'd spent nine thousand dollars to have these three days with her and he'd be damned if he wasn't going to keep her until the last possible second. Maybe he wasn't good enough for Dr. Kris Torrence in real life off of the island, but here she was his and that's all the further he could think for now. When the three days were over he'd worry about the rest. "Take off your shirt. Slowly. I want to watch."

Her eyes widened fractionally. She glanced away and slowly began to unbutton her shirt. The drab cotton garment was buttoned clear up to the neck, so it took her a solid minute of unbuttoning before the shirt finally hung all the way open, exposing her full cleavage to him.

Jack breathed in deeply. His rough hands reached for her breasts, sliding beneath the shirt and gently palming them. She sighed breathily as she closed her eyes.

"Open them," he said firmly as his thumbs began massaging her nipples into stiff peaks. The idea of her thinking about another man made him feel like a possessive animal guarding its territory. His nostrils flared. "I want you to look at me."

Kris slowly opened her eyes.

He massaged her nipples for a solid minute, his cock stiffening as he listened to her soft moans. His hands released her breasts and removed the shirt entirely from her body. She bit her lip as she watched the drab garment fall to the ground.

"Now unzip my pants," he said thickly, his eyelids heavy.

She took a deep breath and blew it out. Slowly, so slowly that he thought his balls would go blue before she finished, she reached for his fly and carefully unzipped it.

Jack's jaw clenched hotly as he slowly backed her up into a corner. "Relax, professor," he murmured. "You know I'd never hurt you."

Kris glanced up at him and held his gaze. After a long, tense moment had passed she nodded—a definitive gesture that made him realize that, in this at least, she trusted him. Oddly, that small gesture got him even hotter, made him want her even more.

When they were in the corner of the hut, he reached up for the black handcuffs, pulling down the lever they were suspended to as he brought them into her line of vision. He saw her eyes go wide, but she said nothing to stop him from continuing.

"Slip into these," he murmured as he held first one and then the other out to her.

She did so hesitantly, gasping when he released his hold on the black velvet handcuffs and the lever went up, bringing her arms high above her head and thrusting out her breasts. Her breathing grew a bit labored as she stared at him wide-eyed, probably wondering how smart she'd been to acquiesce.

Jack's large calloused hands settled at the tops of her breasts, then slowly worked their way down. His eyes narrowed in desire when he heard her breath rush out and felt her nipples further stiffen underneath his palms.

"Get on your knees," he said hoarsely, as he reached for his unzipped trousers and pulled his thick cock out.

Her eyes widened. "But the lever—"

He pressed his palm to her lips. "No questions," he said firmly. "Rule number one: never ask me questions in the bedroom." His eyes grew heavy-lidded. "Just do as you're told," he murmured.

Her nipples visibly tightened even more at his words, the stiff peaks stabbing out for attention. He flicked one back and forth with his index finger, making her groan, and realized that sexually they had been made for each other.

An inexplicable part of him needed this control, this power, in the bedroom. The primitive part of his male brain needed to feel as though he and his cock were being worshipped and longed for, as though both of them were as addicting as drugs. And as though both of them had sexual access to their mate at any time they craved it.

The catch was that Jack had only just recently realized that he didn't want his woman to be docile and worshipping outside of the sexual realm. Which made his little witch perfect for him. The next trick would be getting her to realize the same thing within the next three days.

Jack's eyes narrowed in arousal as he watched her take to her knees, kneeling before him. The lever stretched down to accommodate her, just as he'd known it would. "Put him in your mouth," he said thickly. "Suck on him."

She hesitated for a second, then brought her face level with his erection.

When her full lips closed over the head of his cock, when her eyes closed as she slowly began taking him all the way into her throat, his teeth gritted. He'd never been harder in his life than he was at this moment, watching the woman he'd thought hated him kneel submissively before him and take his cock into her mouth. She was topless and handcuffed, kneeling before him with that deathly tight bun, her cunt still concealed

The Possession

from him by the blue knee-high skirt she wore. Finally—*finally*—he had his professor just as he wanted her.

"Come on, baby," he said hoarsely. "I've been waiting for this for two goddamn years."

Kris hesitated for the briefest of moments then went wild on him. She took him all the way into her mouth until the tip of his manhood reached the back of her throat, then out again. She did it over and over, faster and faster, again and again, deeper and—

Her eyes closed on a groan as she sucked him off, seductive moaning sounds erupting from the back of her throat.

"Oh Jesus," he muttered as he grabbed the back of her head. His nostrils flared when he caught a glimpse of the professor's deathly tight red bun bobbing back and forth as she sucked on him, the prim hairdo more arousing than words could say. "Faster," he gritted out, his breathing increasingly labored. "Make me cum, baby."

She sucked on him faster, concentrating on going up and down the middle of his shaft to the ruby red tip with her lips, sucking his cock up and down, faster and faster. Jack could hear the slurping sounds she was making, the arousing way she kept moaning while she sucked him off. He watched the long, thick length of himself disappear into the warmth of her mouth, over and over, again and again...

He closed his eyes on a growl, his teeth gritting as he spurted his cum inside of her mouth. He groaned as she drained his balls, frantically suckling him while her lips squeezed together to extract all of his juice.

"Keep drinking from him, baby," he said hoarsely, his hips thrusting toward her. His breathing heavy, he cradled her head in close to him, wanting her to devour his cock, much the way a woman wants a man to devour her pussy when he's making her violently cum.

She kept sucking him until his penis was partially flaccid. Only then, when his sporadic breathing had returned to semi-normal and his balls were laying empty nestled under his cock, did her lips begin nibbling at the head, sucking out any remaining cum from the tiny hole.

"Shit," he muttered as her face finally bobbed back up into his line of vision. He reached for her hair and removed the clasp from it. "You're gonna be doing that a lot over the next three days," he promised her on a growl. She said nothing to that, just stared at him with her breasts heaving up and down, waiting for him to issue his next command.

Jack tossed the hair clasp over his shoulder, then came down on one knee to remove the ugly skirt. He took it off quickly, grunting in arrogant pleasure when he noticed she'd kept the black thong on rather than changing back into those god-awful cotton grandma drawers he'd seen in the valise.

He rose up from his knee and took a step back to look his fill at her. His nostrils flared as his dark gaze roamed the length of her body, taking in the heady picture she made. His professor, naked save the black thong, on her knees kneeling before him, her hands suspended above her head with handcuffs, her dark red hair spilling down in a cascade. Just as he'd fantasized for the past two years of one day having her.

He cupped her chin with his hand. "Stand up," he growled, his cock growing erect again already. Sweet Jesus, he'd never gotten this hard this quickly two minutes after emptying his balls. "The first time I fuck you," he murmured, his eyes heavy-lidded as she slowly rose to her feet, "I'm going to mount you from the front so I can watch your beautiful face when I sink into your cunt."

He saw her shiver at that, but she said nothing.

"And then I'm going to fuck you from behind, ramming into you until I cum." His index finger flicked at her erect nipple. "Then I'll feed you and let you get some sleep before I fuck you again," he purred.

The Possession

He saw her swallow slowly as her cat-like green eyes rose up to meet his. She looked nervous, but willing, and he had to wonder why she was still so nervous given the fact she'd just drained him dry.

Maybe, Jack thought on a grunt as he reached up to release the lever so he could tie her to the one above the bed, maybe she'd finally figured out that when the three days were up he was still keeping her...

Her breathing labored, her breasts heaving up and down as she lay completely naked and spread-eagle on the king-sized bed, Kris watched in anticipation as Jack slowly finished undressing before her. She was scared to have sex with him and scared not to have sex with him, but she knew with all certainty that she wanted this time with him. Knew too that there was little to be done about her hesitation at this juncture.

The big bruiser could break her heart if she let him, she realized, so she didn't want to have feelings for him. But she could no sooner stop the way she felt than she could stop the sun from rising in the east or setting in the west.

Emotions are a horrid thing, she decided on a sigh. Especially when you aren't certain of the other person's emotions. And especially when after two years of a tense, battling relationship with the man undressing before you, you come to care for him in a way you hadn't expected.

She likened it to falling in love at first sight with the enemy, to running down a battlefield with guns and grenades in hand, then come to a halt at the last possible second and decide to make love instead of kill each other. That's what this felt like—surreal and unbelievably confusing.

Up until the moment she had donned her professor's garb, which for all intents and purposes where Jack was concerned might as well be battle fatigues, she had carried around this torch of hope that maybe this inexplicable spark between them could extend beyond the island and become something more than what it was when they left this place. But when she'd donned the clothes...

She took a deep breath and blew it out. For the first time, the surreality of the situation had come crashing down on her.

That irritatingly sexy eyebrow of his shot up. "Having second thoughts, professor?" he grumbled. "Because it's a bit too late for that." His jaw clenched as he threw his boxer shorts into the chair her spectacles were laying in. "You're all mine for three days," he growled.

She smiled, which she could tell confused him. "No second thoughts," she whispered as her gaze raked the length of his impressive body. *Just wondering how I'll be able to walk away from you when the three days are done.*

Jack's body was hard and muscled all over, chiseled and sleek in a beautiful, masculine way. His arms were heavy with muscle and vein-roped, his legs solid and proportionately well developed. His chest was the most perfect she'd ever seen, hard with muscle and sexy with a pelt of black hair that tapered downwards to his...

She wet her lips. This was the first look she'd had at his cock since the night in the tiki bar and lordy, lordy it looked even more impressive in good lighting. It was huge—long and thick. And rock-hard. *For her.*

To hell with her worries. Tomorrow could take care of itself.

Kris could scarcely move because of the binds that held her hands suspended over her head. The black handcuffs were now secured to a lever behind the bed, keeping her arms thrust up and back so she couldn't use them at all. Her breathing hitched when she saw Jack's gaze roam over her thrust-up breasts. She shivered when, standing over her, he palmed one, rubbing his thumb over the extended nipple. "Jack," she whispered.

He stilled, enjoying the sound of his name on her lips. "I like you like this, professor," he murmured. "Tied up and waiting for me to fuck you."

He came down on the bed then, settling his heavy body between her splayed thighs. On his knees, he ran his large, calloused palms all over her body, feeling her everywhere, touching everything for as long and as leisurely as he wanted to.

By the time he'd had his fill of touching her, by the time his fingers started playing in her dark red pussy hair, Kris was so turned on she thought she'd die if he didn't fuck her. "Please," she moaned, arching her hips up. She groaned when his thumb began massaging her drenched clit. "Jack, please."

His nostrils flared as he watched her body writhe beneath him. "I like it when you beg," he growled. "Tell me who you want to fuck your cunt, sweetheart, and then I'll think about it."

"You," she groaned, gasping when his other hand tweaked a stiff nipple.

"Say my name."

"Jack McKenna," she unhesitatingly breathed out. She shivered when he thrust one finger inside of her and slowly began pushing it in and out of her. "I want Jack McKenna to fuck me," she said in a rush that sounded half hysterical.

"Anyone else, professor?" he asked arrogantly, bringing the hand that had been massaging her nipple down to her pussy to play with the clit. He continued fucking her with his other hand, adding a second finger to fill her tight cunt up with him.

"No! No other man," she promised as she closed her eyes and enjoyed the feel of having her pussy played in and with. "Jack, please," she whimpered as she threw her hips at him again. "*Please.*"

He rubbed her clit fast and furiously, inducing her to gasp. "Come on, baby," he gritted out, his erection stiff and ready for her. "Cum for daddy."

Kris' eyes flew open at his words, the sound of them much more arousing than they ever would have been coming from Lauren. Jack was just as kinky as the Frenchman and she loved it. "Oh god," she said loudly on a groan, spreading her legs as wide as they could go to give him full access to her drenched flesh. *"I'm coming."*

She burst on a loud moan that would have sounded tortured to anyone not present in the room to witness her pleasure. Her nipples immediately stiffened to the point of aching as blood rushed up to heat her face and erogenous zones. "Oh god," she continued to groan as she frantically thrust her hips at him, wanting impaled deeper and harder on his fingers.

Jack abruptly stopped finger-fucking her, causing her eyes to fly open. She glowered at him.

He grunted. "Don't glare at me, baby," he growled as he settled his heavy body on top of hers. He palmed her breasts, his thumbs running over the stiff nipples until she was gasping again. "I need to fuck your sweet cunt."

He'd never write Hallmark cards, but good lord the man did things to her with words alone that no man had previously been able to accomplish with his hands. "Then fuck me," she whispered. She began thrashing her hands inside of her bindings, wanting out of them. "I need to touch you," she said in a rush. "Please..."

His jaw clenched as he sank his cock balls-deep into her pussy, his teeth gritting when he saw her gasp, saw her head fall back submissively onto the pillows. "That's right, baby," he said thickly as he slowly thrust in and out of her suctioning flesh. "Just lay there and enjoy it. Daddy will do all the work."

Her lips parted slightly on a sigh, the feel of his cock ramming in and out of her pussy coupled with his kinky words highly arousing. She'd never before considered how a single word could cause a woman's clit to pulse and perspiration to dot her brow, but that's exactly what Jack's constant referencing to himself as a forbidden father figure did to her.

Kris moaned, her eyes closing as he picked up the pace and began thrusting harder and deeper inside of her.

"Look at me," he gritted out, sinking balls-deep into her cunt over and over again. She could hear her flesh enveloping him, hear the sound of protest it made on his upstrokes, trying to suction his cock back in, not wanting him to leave.

Still moaning softly, her eyes flicked open and her gaze clashed with his.

"Good girl," he murmured. His jaw was tight, the vein on his neck prominent. "Your pussy feels so good," he said hoarsely as he kept up the steady, even thrusts. He rotated his hips and slammed into her, causing her to gasp. "I'm going to fuck you all night, Krissy, so get used to feeling me inside of you."

"Jack, please," she moaned, her legs wrapping around his hips. She felt half crazed because of the bindings, the urge to touch him overwhelming. "Harder," she begged.

He wanted to slow down, to show her who held the power in their lovemaking as any master would, but in that moment all he could think of was getting deeper and deeper inside of her, of ramming his cock in and out of the sticky, wet flesh he'd coveted for two agonizingly long years.

Jack groaned, his eyelids heavy as he sank fully into her, again and again and again. He fucked her harder and faster, his teeth gritting as their flesh slapped together and the scent of their combined perspiration and arousal reached his nostrils.

Kris' head fell back on a moan, her eyes still open. She noticed the ceiling for the first time...and the mirror that gleamed overhead. The sight of his buttocks clenching as he sank into her cunt, the visual image of having a heavily muscled man's body covering hers while her hands were secured above her head so she couldn't move—

The sight of Jack McKenna fucking Dr. Kris Torrence...

"*Oh god,*" she groaned as she watched Jack ram himself inside of her, as she watched his steely buttocks clench and contract, over and over, again and again. He rotated his hips and slammed into her hard, thrusting faster and deeper, growling as he fucked her.

"*Jack.*"

Her eyes closed on a wail that sounded half delirious and half pleasurous. Her body began to tremble as he mounted her impossibly harder, slamming into her flesh with animalistic thrusts. Her nipples stabbed up into his chest, the friction his chest hair provided her undoing.

"*Oh my god.*" Kris broke on a loud moan, her lower body shaking as she convulsed beneath him, her orgasm ripping through her belly. She frantically threw her hips back at him, gluttonously wanting fucked harder while she came.

"Krissy," Jack gritted out as he squeezed her body tighter to his and gave her the hard pummeling she wanted. He surged faster and faster, sinking deeper and harder into her suctioning flesh, his eyes shutting in a state of near delirium as his orgasm drew closer.

"*My pussy,*" he growled. "*All mine.*"

Jack followed her into orgasm, bursting on a loud groan, his teeth gritting as he spurted his cum deep inside of her. He kept up the mad thrusting, fucking her like an animal, moaning as his balls were drained of seed.

He came for what felt like hours, but realistically could have been only mere seconds. The need to be as close as possible to the woman lying beneath him was as foreign a feeling as it was overwhelming.

"Krissy," he murmured as he slowly came down from his high, as his thrusts gradually winded down, becoming softer and gentler. "Krissy," he said as his eyes opened, and he saw the face of the woman who had haunted his fantasies for two solid years.

Jack threaded both sets of calloused fingers through her hair, further securing her to him. His dark gaze roamed over her face, at last coming to rest at her eyes.

They stared at each other in silence for a protracted moment, both of them too affected and too exhausted to speak. But finally, Kris' eyes gentled and she whispered, "I need to touch you, Jack. Please let me touch you."

His nostrils flared as he stared down at her. "I don't know what you're doing to me, professor," he murmured, "but it's scaring the shit out of me."

With those cryptic words he reached up and released the lever, allowing her arms and hands freedom of movement. He wanted to be touched by her as much as she wanted to touch him.

When her hands found his back and she began to softly stroke him, his tense muscles relaxed. Breathing her scent in deeply, he lowered his face against her neck and, still buried inside of her, fell fast asleep.

Chapter Fourteen

When Kris awoke the next afternoon, it was to the feel of Jack's hard cock sinking into her flesh from behind. He'd taken her that way once before, an hour or so after he'd fallen asleep on top of her last night. He'd sunk into her from behind, again and again, oblivious to anything besides fucking her.

After that he'd fed her food, just as he'd promised he would. Or more to the point, she had fed him food. Jack had laid himself out on the bed, all sprawled out like the king of the castle, while she reclined next to him and fed him whatever he wanted. Occasionally he'd order her to pop her nipple into his mouth, or to massage his balls, or something else of a sexual nature, but for the most part they'd just talked and ate.

When the meal was over, he'd gazed down at her, his eyes heavy-lidded, and murmured that he wanted sucked off again. She'd immediately complied, by then more because she wanted as many memories of him as she could make to take home with her rather than because she was merely giving him what he'd paid for. He'd readily accepted his due, arrogantly lounging on his back with his hands behind his head as she'd sucked him off until he came on a soft groan and fell asleep.

Jack had woken up a few hours later, hornier than hell and wanting more of everything. He'd played with her body in the bed, doing everything and anything he wanted to do to her, his touches arrogant and possessive. He'd sucked on her nipples, played in her pussy, blindfolded and handcuffed her while he'd fucked her every which way imaginable. He'd taken her standing up and sitting down, from the rear and from the front, eventually spewing inside of her while they did it doggy.

He'd taken her so many times and in so many positions that Kris had begun to wonder how the hell one man could cum so much. She had also begun to wonder if maybe, just maybe, Jack was doing his damnedest to store up memories of her too.

She'd fallen asleep hoping, but never really believing it. And now, several hours later, she was given no time to contemplate her thoughts, for Jack was busily mounting her again.

Lying on her belly, his large hands cupping her breasts beneath her, he was thrusting in and out of her with leisurely strokes, appreciative *mmmm* sounds sexily erupting from his throat.

She wiggled her butt to let him know she was awake.

"Mmm," Jack purred, his face coming down closer to her ear. "Get up on your knees and do that for me, baby."

Kris semi-complied, teasing him by rearing her hips up just a bit, but otherwise staying on her belly.

"You want spanked?" he growled as he sat up, his cock leaving her flesh with a suctioning sound. He whacked her on the butt, just enough to make the skin there tingle. "Hell, you probably do," he muttered. "You begged me to do it last night."

She glanced at him from over her shoulder and chuckled, a dimple popping out on either cheek. He studied her dimples broodingly, his hands massaging her ass.

"Mmm," she said dreamily, her eyes closing as she rested her face on her arm. "That feels so nice."

He grunted. "Some sex slave you're turning out to be. I think we need to reverse positions here."

She grinned, her eyes still closed. "Well, seeing as how you spent nine thousand dollars to be sexually catered to for two more days, you're probably right."

Jack stilled. "Two more days," he muttered. He said something else under his breath, but it was incoherent.

Kris' eyes opened. Her forehead wrinkled. "Did you say something?" she asked throatily, her voice still groggy from slumber.

"What? No," he grumbled. He took a deep breath, and then changed the subject by whacking her on the butt again. She yelped. "On your knees, professor. I want your face down and your ass up." He ran a calloused palm over the red spot on her buttocks that his small spanking had made. "You know it's my favorite position," he murmured.

The arousal in his voice immediately aroused her as well. She drew up to her knees, her flesh already wetting for him again, and did as he'd instructed her to do—ass up, face down.

With no preliminaries, Jack sank into her on a groan. "Oh shit," he muttered, grabbing her hips as he slowly began to thrust in and out of her from behind. "I love how your pussy is always wet and ready for me."

And she loved how perfect he felt inside of her, how beautiful and desirable he made her feel. Jack looked at her and touched her as though he couldn't get enough of her, as though she was the only woman he wanted. Even during the initial wild days of the excursion, she'd never seen his eyes straying toward another woman. A bunch of gorgeous, naked women had been strolling around ready and willing, but his sole focus had been on obtaining her.

Kris felt tears gathering in her eyes and blinked them away. There would be time for wallowing in self-pity when she returned to San Francisco—plenty of time in fact. But this time was for Jack, and for creating as many memories of him as she could.

She roughly threw her hips back at him, arching her ass up as high as it could go.

Jack purred, his fingers digging into her hips. "You want it hard, professor?" he asked arrogantly. She was certain if she could see him his jaw would be clenched. "Well so do I," he growled.

He took her like an animal then, pistoning in and out of her flesh in deep, hard, fast strokes, groaning while his hands held onto her hips. His teeth gritted as he rode her hard, as he sank again and again into her welcoming cunt. The sound of flesh smacking against flesh filled the room, the scent of their combined arousal permeated the air.

"Jack," she moaned, throwing her hips at him faster. "Deeper—harder," she panted. She couldn't make up her mind what she wanted, just knew that she needed him to impale her as hard and as fast and as deep as was humanly possible, or maybe humanly impossible.

"Come on, baby," he gritted out, surging inside of her again and again. "Throw that pussy at me."

He went wild on her, pummeling her animalistically from behind, groaning as he felt his orgasm draw near. "Shit," he muttered, unable to hold it back, wanting to wait for Krissy to come first. But the need to spurt inside of her was overwhelming.

Jack's eyes closed tightly, the vein in his neck bulging, as his fingers dug into the flesh of her hips. He sank into her balls-deep, once, twice, three times more, then, teeth gritting, groaned as he spurted his cum deep inside of her.

She kept throwing her hips back at him, draining him while he growled. "Give me all of your cum, Jack," she moaned, loving that she had this affect on him. "All of it."

He did. And she felt sexy because of it.

"I'm sorry," he said gruffly as he slowly came down from the high, a surly tone of voice she'd finally come to understand was just how Jack was and not meant to be mean to her. He stroked in and out a few times more to completely drain himself. "I need to rest for a few minutes," he said tiredly.

Kris smiled when his heavy body possessively covered hers, his massive arms coming around to either side of her head to rest as he pressed her torso down with his larger one.

"I don't mind," she whispered in all honesty. "I just like lying here with you like this."

He grunted, an arrogant sound that made her grin. "Me too," he grumbled.

Five minutes later, he was snoring contentedly. And Kris was wondering if maybe, just maybe, surreality and reality could become one.

If the Whos down in Who-ville and the Grinch could work things out, then maybe Dr. Kris Torrence and Jack McKenna could too.

* * * * *

By the time their last night together arrived, Kris was certain that even Jack could feel their impending separation. He wouldn't let her out of his sight, practically wouldn't even let her out of the bed.

They made love and they talked, they drank expensive wine and ate expensive food. But mostly they made love. Even when Jack wasn't penetrating her, he was still fondling her, or instructing her to fondle him.

"Massage my balls while you feed me," he murmured. His head fell back on the oversized padded chair they were lounging together on, his eyes closing in fatigue. He grunted arrogantly when he felt her hand cup his balls and begin to gently knead them.

Kris massaged his tight sac with one hand and popped pieces of prime rib into his mouth with the other.

"Mmmm," Jack purred, his eyes remaining closed as he chewed on the steak.

She grinned, wondering if the appreciative sound was due to the food or the fondling. She knew, of course, it was a combination of both. "I agree," she murmured. "It's an excellent cut of beef." She drew the hand that was massaging his tight balls up to his erection long enough to squeeze it.

Jack opened one eye. "Witch," he muttered. He closed his eye, enjoying the feel of her hand when she resumed massaging his scrotum. "You've been draining me left and right and still want more," he teased, sounding his usual arrogant and surly self.

"And more and more and more."

His dark eyes opened and found hers. "Then what are you waiting for, baby?" he murmured. "Climb into daddy's lap."

Kris bit her lip. Damn if he didn't get her wet every time he referred to himself in such a wicked way...

She turned herself around so she straddled his lap, one of her hands coming up to rest on his shoulder, the other one grabbing his thick shaft by the base. She guided the tip of his cock to the entrance of her flesh, groaning when she sank down onto him, fully impaling his shaft within her.

"Mmm yeah," he purred.

Jack reached for her breasts, softly stroking them with the backs of his calloused hands as she rode him slowly, tenderly. Neither one of them were in the mood for a fast and furious mating, but rather for a slow and seductive lovemaking session.

"You feel so good," Jack said thickly, his eyelids heavy. "Your pussy feels like it was made for me." He buried his face into her chest, drew a nipple into his mouth, and suckled it.

Kris closed her eyes and hugged him tightly while she slowly, rhythmically, rode up and down his cock. Those damn tears were stinging the backs of her eyes again and she refused to let them fall.

For now, for this glorious moment in time, Jack McKenna belonged to her. Somehow, it would have to be enough.

Something emotional inside of her broke, some spring that uncoiled and demanded she live for the moment and take as many memories as she could with her. She withdrew her nipple from his mouth and rode him hard then, bobbing up and down on his lap, impaling herself with his cock faster and deeper.

"Krissy," he said hoarsely, his hands reaching around to palm and knead her buttocks. "Oh god, Krissy."

Kris rode him frantically, desperately, never wanting the moment to end. She moaned and groaned as she sank down onto him, greedily wanting his cock buried inside of her as deep as it could go.

When it was over, when Jack shouted out his satisfaction and came, she watched the way his teeth gritted, memorized the way his jaw clenched…

And knew that as long as she lived she'd never see a more beautiful sight than Jack coming inside of her.

Chapter Fifteen

When the third and final day was complete, and the time to leave the island was at hand, Kris felt as though her heart might break in two. There were a million and one things she wanted to say to Jack, and a million and one more ways she wanted to make love with him.

By the time she began donning her professor clothing, the actions of the past three days were making themselves felt. Her nipples ached from being sucked on, her pussy was sore from having Jack's cock constantly buried inside of her, and her clit was overly sensitive from being sucked on more times than she could count.

And yet she still wanted more—and more and more and more.

With a sunken heart, she silently admitted to herself that all vacations have to come to an end. And that's what this excursion had been, a vacation. In real life Jack could afford to date, and chose to date, perfectly gorgeous women with perfect bodies—not passingly pretty women with imperfect bodies.

Kris sighed as she tossed the black handcuffs into her valise. She wanted to have an intimate souvenir of the hedonistic nights they'd spent together and the black handcuffs were about as intimate of a reminder as she could think to take with her.

Her eyes flew to the knotted pine bureau. She smiled nostalgically as she walked over to it and picked up her spectacles. She thought back on last night when Jack had teased her about them.

"These are the ugliest glasses I've ever seen, professor." He held them up as if studying them. "Where'd you buy them? Nerds-R-Us?"

She looked up from her crème brulee long enough to chuckle. "Actually at Geeks-R-Us," she teased him back. "There's a distinct difference between the two, you know."

He grunted, setting them back down on the bureau before joining her at the small, intimate table in the hut.

She smiled. After that they'd talked and they'd talked. They'd discussed everything and nothing, speaking on topics as diverse as San Francisco's art scene, university politics, and the city politics he often had to sort through to benefit McKenna Construction.

"I don't regret buying the company," Jack admitted, digging into his own dessert. They were both naked and very comfortable being that way with each other. "But basically I'm a works-with-his-hands kinda guy. I dislike dealing with all that other bullshit."

She smiled. "And you're very, very good at working with your hands," she said sexily. It amazed her how seductive she could be where Jack was concerned. Before Jack had charged into her life she'd felt about as seductive as the bearded lady at the circus.

That eyebrow of his shot up. "Come here, professor," he murmured...

Kris sighed, smiling to herself as she absently toyed with her spectacles. Snapping out of it, she shook her head slightly, then threw them into the valise.

"Hey professor," Jack grumbled as he strode into the hut. "Your plane awaits you."

She turned on her heel, her heart simultaneously thumping and constricting when she saw him. He was dressed in another Italian business suit. She guessed that he probably had a meeting to attend later in the day or something.

Kris smiled at him fully, even though she felt like she was dying on the inside. "Thank you for letting me know, Jack."

She took a deep breath, and then nodded. "I guess I should be on my way then."

Jack studied her broodingly, but didn't say anything to waylay her departure. "I guess so," he muttered. He sighed, running a hand over his jaw. "Thanks for everything, professor," he said in the gentlest tone of voice she'd ever heard him use. "I had the best three nights of my life with you."

She wanted to cry. She also wanted to tell him that they could have many more nights that were just as wonderful. She smiled instead, nodding again. "Me too," she whispered.

Kris took a deep breath, fearing she might do something completely embarrassing like tear up. She blinked a few times in rapid succession before extending her hand to Jack. "Thanks for everything. I'll see you at the university, I'm sure."

Jack looked at her hand, but didn't take it. He took a deep breath instead, then drew her close and hugged her tightly.

Kris closed her eyes just as tightly, determined not to cry. Luckily he couldn't see her face, so he couldn't know how close she was.

"I'll definitely see you at the university, Krissy," he murmured into her hair. "And you better not avoid me like you used to."

She smiled, her eyes still closed. "I won't," she promised. "Avoid you that is."

"Good."

Jack gave her one of his bear hugs, a gesture she loved as much as his lovemaking. "Take care of yourself," he said gruffly.

"I will."

When he released her, Kris took a steadying breath, picked up her valise, and smiled brilliantly up to him, a dimple popping out on either cheek. "Goodbye, Jack."

He nodded, his dark eyes studying her face. He memorized her dimples, her cat-like green eyes. "Goodbye, Krissy."

Chapter Sixteen
One week later

𝕊

She was miserable without him. A week had already came and went and every day, every hour, had grown more unbearable than the last. She wanted to see him, to touch him, to hear him growl and grunt at her. Anything. Any contact would be welcomed contact.

Kris sighed, then shoved another spoonful of chocolate ice cream between her lips as she watched the ending of her new favorite movie—*How The Grinch Stole Christmas*.

"Don't fall for it, Cindy-Lou," she muttered to the screen as the reformed Grinch served up the Christmas feast to the Whos. "The damn man will wine you and dine you with who-pudding and rare who-roast-beast, and then he'll leave you, cleaving your heart in two."

She frowned. "God, I'm pathetic," she mumbled. "It's been a week and he hasn't come for you, Kris. He's not ever going to come for you—get it through your head already."

Flicking off the television set, Kris stood up with a sigh, and then plodded into the kitchen to put her ice cream bowl into the sink.

It was time to move on. It was time to stop obsessing over Jack.

* * * * *

He was miserable without her. A week had already came and went and every day, every hour, had grown more unbearable than the last. He wanted to see her, to touch her, to growl and grunt at her. Anything. Any contact would be welcomed contact.

Jack sighed, then shoved another spoonful of chocolate ice cream between his lips as he watched the ending of his new favorite movie—*The Nutty Professor.*

"Don't fall for it," he muttered to the screen as the professor took the only woman he coveted out on a date. "The damn woman will let you wine her and dine her with prime rib and crème brulee, and then she'll leave you, cleaving your heart in two."

He frowned. "God, I'm pathetic," he mumbled. "It's been a week and she hasn't come for you, Jack. She's not ever going to come for you—get it through your head already."

Flicking off the television set, Jack stood up with a sigh, and then plodded into the kitchen to put his ice cream bowl into the sink.

It was time to move on. It was time to stop obsessing over Krissy.

* * * * *

"I can't stop thinking about him!" Kris dramatically wailed, bemoaning the fates that had conspired against her. "He's in my every thought, my every…" She waved an impatient hand. "My every everything."

Her friend chuckled, the single mother of an adorable blue-eyed, golden haired baby boy shaking her head in disapproval. "So go tell him how you feel. How do you know he isn't feeling the same way if you don't tell him how you feel?"

Kris frowned as she fell into her chair. "He's too good for me," she mumbled. "He's a thousand times more good-looking than I am." She sighed. "He'd never want a woman like me for keeps."

Her friend sighed too, glancing away. Her eyes were remote, distant, as if remembering a long ago moment in time she preferred to keep sealed away. "There was a man once..." She smiled, still looking away. "A man I loved. But I was too scared to tell him how I felt and too scared to ask him how he felt." Her friend glanced up, at last meeting her gaze. "I've always regretted it," she said quietly. "Because I've lost him forever."

Kris' eyes widened. "Why don't you try to find him?"

Her friend was quiet for a long moment, but eventually she shook her head. "We weren't meant to be," she said softly. "We just weren't meant to be."

* * * * *

"I can't stop thinking about her!" Jack dramatically wailed, bemoaning the fates that had conspired against him. "She's in my every thought, my every..." He waved an impatient hand. "My every everything."

His best friend John Calder chuckled, his blue-eyed, golden haired head shaking in disapproval. "So go tell her how you feel. How do you know she isn't feeling the same way if you don't tell her how you feel?"

Jack frowned as he fell into his chair. "She's too good for me," he mumbled. "She's a thousand times smarter and more good-looking than I am." He sighed. "She'd never want a man like me for keeps."

John sighed too, glancing away. His eyes were remote, distant, as if remembering a long ago moment in time he preferred to keep sealed away. "There was a woman once..." He smiled, still looking away. "A woman I loved. But I was too scared to tell her how I felt and too scared to ask her how she felt." John glanced up, at last meeting his gaze. "I've always regretted it," he said quietly. "Because I've lost her forever."

Jack's eyes widened. "Why don't you try to find her?"

John was quiet for a long moment, but eventually he shook his head. "We weren't meant to be," he said softly. "We just weren't meant to be."

Chapter Seventeen

ಶಾ

"Good morning, Dr. Torrence."

"Good morning, Dr. Moore."

Kris frowned as she strolled into the faculty lounge, her surly mood evident. She was dressed in a conservative navy business skirt that ended at the knee, a white cotton shirt that was buttoned all the way to the top, and her mass of dark red curls was secured in a tight bun at the nape of her neck. Completing her usual ensemble was a pair of black spectacles perched at the tip of her nose.

Clearly, she felt about as good as she looked. But then she'd never placed much importance on fashion anyway.

Kris inclined her head to Dr. Moore as she plodded by him, feeling as glum as glum could be. "How are you doing today?" she asked conversationally. "I'm sorry I'm late." *I was busy brooding over the Grinch!* "Has anything happened around here I should know about?"

Dr. Moore nodded, his pompous tone as annoying as it had ever been. "Quite a bit actually…"

She listened to her colleague's rather long-winded answer with half an ear as she poured herself a cup of what most people would call beans and water, but what the university called, or tried to pass off as at any rate, coffee.

Kris ignored Dr. Moore as she sipped from the steamy mug of cheap quasi-Columbian brew, and reflected back on the conversation she'd had with her friend last night. Maybe she had been right. Maybe she should tell Jack how she felt.

"Oh," Dr. Moore continued, breaking her out of her reverie, "I almost forgot to mention that Mr. McKenna is in your office." He shook his head, perturbed. "He's waiting to speak to you," he said disdainfully as he adjusted his tie.

Kris' heartbeat began to race. "Mr. McKenna? As in Jack McKenna?" She swallowed roughly as she looked at her colleague, her eyes wide. Could it possibly be true? "Are you certain?"

"Afraid so."

"Did he say what he wants?" she breathed out.

"Why don't you ask him yourself," a dark voice growled from behind her.

Kris whipped around, almost spilling her coffee at her surprise as she did so. Dr. Moore cleared his throat uncomfortably while nervously readjusting his tie. "Jack," she breathed out. She shook her head slightly, remembering that Dr. Moore was in the room. "You wanted to see me, Mr. McKenna?"

"Hell, yes, I want to see you," he growled. He jabbed a finger in the general direction of her office door. "Let's go talk, lady."

Kris frowned severely, but smiled on the inside. Jack was here! He'd come back! If even just to growl at her...

As soon as they reached her modest office, and the door was shut firmly behind them, she turned to look at him, smiling as she drank in the sight of him. She knew she should probably play it cool, but good lord he looked wonderful to her Jack-starved senses. "How are you?" she asked, wanting to know everything. "It's so good to see you."

His jaw clenched as his dark gaze broodingly raked over her face. "Is it, Krissy?" he grumbled.

She blinked. "Well, of course." She shook her head. "I've missed you, Jack," she admitted, deciding to be honest about at least that much. She'd been so hungry for his presence that all of a sudden she no longer cared how much of a fool she made of herself. "I've missed you a lot."

Jack's eyes narrowed suspiciously. "You know what I'm up to and you're trying to throw me off the scent, aren't you?" His nostrils flared when she gazed at him as though she had no idea what he was talking about. "Well it won't work," he growled.

Jack grunted—music to her ears!—then whipped out a large envelope she hadn't noticed him carrying under his arm. He briskly opened the envelope, pulling photographs of her out of it. Photographs, she noticed when he placed them on the desk, that were of her at Hotel Atlantis—naked and smiling on Jack's lap while he held her labial lips apart with his calloused fingers.

Kris' heart sank while her pulse simultaneously sped up. She felt as though she was going to be sick. "You're here to blackmail me?" she whispered, her stomach and heart painfully knotting. "That's why you're here?"

He nodded, his jaw clenched. "That's right, professor. You can either accept my conditions and have a long, prosperous career, or you can turn down my conditions and accept the consequences."

She glanced away, wanting to be alone so badly she could cry. In fact, she wanted to be alone so she could cry. "I see," she said quietly, her voice monotone. "And what are your conditions?"

As if she cared. She didn't care about anything anymore.

"Marry me," he whispered.

Her head shot up. Her heart began thumping wildly against her chest. Surely she hadn't heard him correctly... "What?" she breathed out.

Jack's dark gaze bore into hers. And for the first time in two years he looked vulnerable to her. "I said marry me." He glanced away, sighing as he pinched the bridge of his nose for a threadbare second. "I know you're too good for me..."

She could only gape.

His hand left the bridge of his nose as he turned back to glare at her. "And I know you don't love me the way I love you…"

She was going to faint. She was certain she was going to faint.

"But I'll take what I can get." His jaw clenched as his hand slashed definitively through the air. "I need to be with you, Krissy, and I don't care how manipulative I have to be to get you."

Jack shook his head, looking more resigned than she'd ever seen him. "I'm miserable without you," he said quietly. "I'm sorry I have to do this to you, Krissy, but I promise I'll be the best husband on earth. I—"

"Oh Jack shut up! Of course I'll marry you!" Kris flung herself at him with such force that the big bruiser grunted at the impact. She wrapped her arms around his middle and hugged tightly, smiling like a doofus. "I've been so miserable without you that all I've done since I left the island is eat chocolate ice cream, watch television, and whine to my best friend."

"Me too," he growled as he put his arms around her and squeezed. "John is sick to death of my bitching," he admitted on a grumble. His face fell to her hair and he breathed in the scent of it. "Goddamn, I've missed you," he said hoarsely. "I love you so much, Krissy."

"Oh Jack, I love you too." She held onto him tightly, her eyes closed and her lips smiling.

"Thank God you caved easily," he sighed, mumbling as if to himself. "I was afraid I was going to have to pull out the big guns and quote Kenny Rogers."

She didn't know what he meant by that, and didn't particularly care, so she let the enigmatic statement go right on by, too overjoyed to give it any thought.

Jack ran his hands over her backside, then rotated his hips to let her know his erection was there and seeking attention.

"Come on, professor," he growled, reaching under her skirt. "It's time for daddy to get you out of those grandma drawers."

She chuckled as she gazed up at him. "I'm wearing a black thong," she admitted. "I burned the grandma drawers."

"Well goddamn," he drawled as his hands found the thong in question and he pulled it down, letting it drop to the floor. "I always knew you were made for me."

She unzipped his trousers, nodding her agreement. "And I always knew that you were made for me."

Jack plopped her down on the desk, grunting like a Neanderthal when she spread her thighs wide for him. Her pussy was already wet and waiting—just like he liked it. Then again, he liked Krissy's pussy any way he could get it.

"And that's not all," he growled. "You're not just gonna marry me. You're gonna have my kid too," he announced as he guided his cock to her opening. "It's time to work on Junior, sweetheart," he said through gritted teeth as he plunged his cock deep inside of her, his nostrils flaring when her wet flesh immediately enveloped him, suctioning him in.

Kris gasped, clinging to him. "You want a baby already?"

"Already?" he groaned, sliding in and out of the flesh he'd missed so damn badly. "I'm over forty, baby. It's now or it's never."

She grinned and then groaned, her head falling back as he picked up the pace of his thrusting. "Now," she moaned.

He grunted arrogantly, liking the idea of putting his baby in her belly. "I love you, Krissy," Jack rasped out as he plunged deep inside of her. "I'll always love you."

Kris smiled, happier than she'd ever thought to be. "I love you too, Jack. Always." She cupped his face with her palms. "You're lucky you came to get me, you big bruiser. I was giving you one more day and then I was coming after you myself."

"It woulda been a short walk," Jack unabashedly admitted. "I was camped out in front of your place with binoculars every night this past week making sure no man touched what's mine."

Kris threw her head back and laughed, then moaned when he began taking his thrusting seriously. "Never," she promised on a half moan, half wail. "For the rest of my life there will never be any man for me but you, Jack McKenna."

Jack made love to her on the desk, and then again every day for the rest of forever. Surreality had become reality, and reality had become something more beautiful and enduring than either of them had ever thought they'd have.

They married two weeks later on the island they'd fallen in love on. Nine months later, Jack Jr. was born, and one month after that they moved with their son and their five cats to the Fantasy Island John Calder had created from the ashes of Hotel Atlantis.

And then the Grinch and the Nutty Professor lived happily ever after.

THE ADDICTION

Dedication

To Laurann for her endless encouragement, her generosity with midnight cupcakes and Frappuccinos, and the Tokyo story that always gives me a giggle…thanks, Raymond! ;-) And to Giselle for her unending inspiration. It took me years to find the right heroine for John Calder; one phone call to you and she popped into my head as though she'd always been there. Enjoy those stilettos!

Chapter One

"Come on, Lynette, be a friend. I need this job!"

"Shel—"

"Don't say it! Do not say I'm fired! I'll try harder. I promise!"

"It's not a matter of trying harder, honey. I don't think there are enough pole dancing classes in the world to help you. I love you to death, but you are the worst stripper I've come across in over fifteen years in the business."

Shelli Rodgers watched Lynette wear a hole in the carpet as her friend and boss frenetically paced back and forth. A cigarette dangled from Lynette's Botox-injected lips as she strutted around in her well-manicured, and very black, office.

Shelli paused, momentarily distracted from the guillotine that loomed over her head. She supposed the black walls, plush ebony carpet, and dark-as-midnight ceiling were an accurate reflection of Lynette's current and usual abysmal state of mind, but how could anybody like this much black? It was depressing.

"Look," Shelli began, her violet eyes beseeching. She ran a hand through her dark-brown hair, which seemed light in comparison to the office. She moved toward Lynette. "I know everything you say is true, but I—*oomph!*"

She could hear Lynette's long-suffering sigh as Shelli picked herself up from the floor. She winced, realizing that faux pas wasn't about to win her boss over. Why did the chairs have to be the same color as everything else in this wretched room? Damn it.

"You see!" Lynette's nostrils widened as she threw her hands up in dismay. "This is exactly what I'm talking about. You have the grace and coordination of a drunken hyena trying to make its way across a high wire! I've seen full-body vomiting that's more attractive."

"I'm not that bad," Shelli said, frowning.

"Yes!" Lynette shrieked, still pacing. "Yes you are!"

"Okay, maybe I am!" Shelli straightened to her full five feet ten inches, which would have been five feet four inches without benefit of the stripper stilettos she wore. Or tried to wear. "But I still need this job. I really, really need it." How *did* Lynette keep that cigarette's long ash from breaking off and falling onto the carpet? Had it been Shelli, the fire department would have already been dispatched. "Another six months and I'll have my Ph.D. in Anthropology. You'll be rid of me forever, I promise!"

Six months. All Shelli needed was six lousy months and she'd never have to impose upon their friendship again. If there was another job she could work making the same money for the same scant hours per week, she would have moved on long ago. But there wasn't. Not even the world's worst stripper made bad tips. Unless the club patrons demanded their money back, of course. But that had only happened a few times.

Lynette tugged in a long, seemingly cathartic drag of the cigarette. The damn ash still dangled.

"Please," Shelli implored, her violet gaze desperate. "Just one more chance?"

Lynette sighed. She moved the cigarette from her lips to the first two fingers of her left hand. Shelli watched in amazement as the ash held firm.

"All right," Lynette ground out. "One more chance. But this is it, Shel." Her eyes narrowed. "I mean it."

Shelli smiled, relieved and elated. "You won't regret it!"

"I somehow doubt that."

The Addiction

She ignored the slight. "I'm sorry about tonight. I didn't mean to fall into Mr. Rivera."

"Falling into him wasn't the problem," Lynette said, exasperated. "Falling into him and knocking a burning-hot cup of coffee onto his lap was the problem!"

"It couldn't have been too hot," Shelli muttered, her cheeks going up in flames. "It also splattered onto his friend's lap and his friend didn't complain."

"That's because he couldn't feel it! He sits in that wheelchair because his legs are paralyzed, not because it's the latest trend in men's fashion!"

"Maybe it should be," Shelli sniffed, feeling defensive. "The chair matched his suit quite nicely."

Lynette looked ready to strangle her. Perhaps it was time to shut up.

"Thanks again," Shelli enthused, smiling cheerfully. "I'll practice on the pole before work tomorrow." She made her way to the office door, this time without tripping. "See? I'm getting better already."

The cigarette was back in her boss's mouth. Lynette's eyes closed as her hands moved to her temples, rubbing them.

"Did something give you a headache? You should take some aspirin."

Lynette's eyes flew open. The ash broke and fell to the carpet.

"Right," Shelli squeaked. She swallowed heavily. "I'll see you tomorrow."

Chapter Two

He was tired.

His life, his business ventures, his houses, his cars, his women, his friends—all of it.

Friends, he breathed, his hands fisting and unballing at his knees. A better word would be users. Or vultures.

He only had one real friend in this world and that was Jack McKenna. It felt like ages since they'd hung out together and in truth, probably would be ages before they could again. At least they were tentatively scheduled to have a drink together tomorrow while John was on the mainland. *Scheduled!* What had life become when it's necessary to schedule a drink with your best buddy?

That was the shitty part about growing up and becoming adults. Too much work and no time to appreciate the fruits of your labor.

John Calder sat in the back of his limousine, his blue gaze absently staring out the window. Nothing gave him joy anymore. Nothing.

Once upon a time he had aspired to great wealth. He had long ago obtained it. Once upon a time he had set out to be so powerful a man that he could have any famous woman he desired. He'd had them all, a few times.

The problem with dreams, John decided, is that once you fulfilled them there was nothing left to inspire you, no reason to get out of bed in the morning, no new challenges waiting to be conquered. Every new day becomes as monotonous as the one before it, every superficial woman as boring as her predecessor.

His cell phone rang, snagging his attention from the San Francisco landscape whizzing by outside the vehicle. He glanced at the caller ID.

"Daisy Renee Halcomb," he muttered, tossing the cell phone onto the unoccupied space next to him. "Emmy-winning actress now setting her sights on Broadway. I've got news for you, Daisy, you're not talented enough for Broadway."

Nobody was there to listen to his ranting so it didn't matter how unapologetically truthful he was. "You're not only boring, but vain as well."

She could give a decent blowjob, though. Daisy Renee should have set her sights on low-budget porn or on working at John's *Hotel Atlantis* resort. At least then she stood a reasonable chance at not getting booed off stage.

The window separating chauffeur from passenger glided down. John arched an inquisitive dark-gold eyebrow at his driver of ten years. Manuel was a good guy and, John admitted, a good friend. Because of their age gap, their relationship was more like father-and-son than a friendship in the conventional sense, but the older man was good people and John could always rely on him.

"You sure you want to hit the clubs right away? You should eat," Manuel chastised.

John sighed. "No choice, Manny. We're short three girls."

Manuel returned his look with an arched brow of his own. The man understood him too well.

"I know there's still plenty of time, but what the hell else do I have to do? Never mind, don't answer that."

There was no encouraging reply to be stated, after all. John had nothing to do and they both knew it. Work was all John Calder had. Forty years old and he still had no wife and children to go home to, nobody special to grow old with.

You brought this on yourself. Your entire world is of your own making.

John ignored his thoughts and looked back out the window. At least he had his work. That was worth something.

Or it used to be, anyway.

* * * * *

His blue gaze flicked up to the neon-lit marquee. *Venus Rising*. Yep, this was the place Jack had told him about. The best strippers in California, he'd promised.

A small smile tugged at John's lips. His buddy Jack's idea of a great stripper was any woman who'd show him her tits. Still, it was worth checking out. God knows he'd been to almost every other club in the state at one time or another.

Manuel opened the front door to the establishment. The familiar scent of booze and smoke wafted into their faces like a cloud.

"You coming in, Manny?" John inquired, already knowing the answer.

Manuel shook his head. "I'll stay with the car."

John nodded. "Hopefully this will be quick. We can grab a beer afterward."

"Best offer I've had all night."

"I somehow doubt that, with pretty Angelina waiting for you at home," John replied, "but nice try."

Manuel's chuckle made him smile again. Two smiles in one night. It had to be a record.

Making his way past the club's entrance, John paid the requisite cover charge and continued deeper into *Venus Rising*. The pulsating sound of techno-pop music blared loudly, the frenzied beat in tune with the strobe lights. An expensive fog machine worked overtime, giving the club a vampirish feel. It must have been the vibe the establishment's owner had been going for. All the topless barmaids sported gothic, cupless bustiers, leather G-strings and, he noticed as he squinted for a better look, fangs.

Vampires. He rolled his eyes. So overdone.

A well-dressed bouncer of John's acquaintance nodded at him, beckoning for him to come closer. He couldn't remember the guy's name, but recognized his face as that of a former employee. The man had left John's private island in good standing. If memory served, the bouncer's mother had become ill and he'd found it too difficult to commute back and forth from the mainland to the island on an ongoing basis.

Funny. He could recall all those details, but couldn't remember the man's name.

"Mr. Calder," the bouncer said, smiling. "It's me, Mike. You remember?"

Everything but your name. "Of course. How have you been? How is your mother?"

The bouncer seemed surprised that John would remember any details about his life. But then, most people assumed the controversial John Calder was an arrogant, unfeeling asshole concerned with nobody's welfare but his own.

He supposed they had good reason to assume it. Despite his numerous business holdings and vast wealth that sprang from a sophisticated stock portfolio, it was his notorious role as what amounted to a pimp that kept his name in the media.

Hotel Atlantis was situated on John's lush, private island off the coast of San Francisco, just far enough into international waters to make prostitution legal. The women in his employ could hardly be thought of as streetwalkers, though, for they made enviable sums of money that would make most CEOs blush. John kept them well-protected, provided them with the world's richest gentlemen clientele and looked after their well-being in an almost fatherly fashion. But no matter how nicely he dressed it up, he was still a pimp.

That title didn't used to bother him. Lately, it disturbed him a lot.

"My mom's doing real good," Mike said, smiling. "She has her bad days, but she's a fighter. The cancer's in remission."

"I'm very happy to hear that."

Mike inclined his head. "The VIP section is over here. Come on, I'll get you a private table."

"Thank you."

Again the bouncer seemed surprised. This time because of two simple words—*thank you*. Mike looked at John as though he was no longer certain who he was.

Did I come across that bad back then? Was I so caught up in making the next business deal that I forgot basic manners?

Probably, John conceded. Up until about six or seven months ago it had always been about the money.

Mike led him to a private viewing area toward the front of the club. He nodded his thanks at the bouncer before seating himself at the secluded table. If there was one good thing that had come of his infamous reputation, it was that John Calder always got the best seat in the house no matter where he was.

"Mike says you're a bourbon man." Lost in his thoughts, John almost didn't hear or notice the barmaid who stood over him. He glanced up, her bared tits at his eye level. "So here's a bourbon on the house, Mr. Calder. Compliments of the owner, Lynette Shofield."

John's assessing gaze raked over her bared breasts. Her nipples plumped up at his perusal. "Please thank Ms. Shofield for me," he murmured. He lifted the glass. "Cheers."

The barmaid wet her lips. "Cheers." She thrust her breasts closer to his face. "Holler if you need me," she said thickly.

John nodded then looked away. She wanted to fuck him. No surprise there. She had been told who he was, after all.

Chapter Three
ಸ಄

High heels in hand, Shelli jogged toward *Venus Rising* as quickly as her tennis shoes could carry her. Time had gotten away from her back at San Francisco State. She'd been so embroiled in writing up her proposal for the dissertation committee that the passing hours had felt more like minutes.

Lynette would not be pleased. Ordinarily her boss didn't mind when she was running a little late on account of her university classes, but Shelli reasoned every mistake she made tonight would likely grate on Lynette's nerves after last evening's hot-coffee fiasco. Not to mention the fact that Shelli had promised to practice on the pole before the club even opened.

No. Lynette definitely would not be a happy camper.

I wish I didn't need this job. I wish Lindsay would get her head out of her ass and help Mom make ends meet until I graduate!

Shelli exhaled as she ran full throttle ahead. Maybe it wasn't fair to even semi-blame her sister for the mess Dad's death had left the whole family in, but now that he was gone, everyone needed to pitch in and help. Shelli hated working at *Venus Rising* as much as Lynette hated employing her, but she was doing what needed to be done. Not that Shelli wanted Lindsay working alongside her, getting groped by drunk, ugly men, but hell, even a part-time job at McDonald's would have gone a long way toward helping the family out.

Lindsay had always been the self-involved sister, the one so tightly wrapped up in herself that it was a wonder she could breathe. But despite that flaw, she had never been one to turn her back on the family when they needed her, either. Her behavior since their father's death was unpredictable at best and shameful at worst.

"Hey, watch where you're going!"

"Careful, bitch!"

Shelli ignored the belligerent shouts of the people she'd accidentally barreled into and kept running. If they hadn't been so nasty, she would have taken the time to stop and apologize, but their attitudes made them unworthy of further tardiness from work. Lynette would be pissed enough.

Six more months, Shel. You can hang in there for six damn months. And when it's over, you will never look back.

* * * * *

Boring. The only word that came to mind to describe *Venus Rising* was boring.

John sighed, wondering not for the first time if he'd simply become too jaded. All of the girls were pretty enough, some might even say beautiful. Yet none of them had managed to snag his attention, let alone pique his curiosity.

"You're here to find hookers," he muttered to himself, picking up his bourbon to finish it, "not a fucking soul mate."

The music changed and a new trio of dancers appeared on stage, each of them working their own pole. Two fanged blondes and one fanged brunette. John rolled his eyes, quickly tiring of the vampire theme.

The blondes were typical strippers, their routines in sync and well-rehearsed. They looked good, danced beautifully, and still he felt nothing. Depressed, he decided it was time to quietly make his exit. Maybe a good night's sleep would put him in a better mood. Assuming he could fall asleep. Insomnia had been his constant companion for months now.

John stood to leave, then paused as a loud *boom* snagged his attention. He glanced up at the stage, immediately noticing that the stripper working the middle pole—the brunette—had taken a fall. Instinctively he took a step toward her to help, but stopped as she stood up and continued gyrating as though nothing had happened.

One eyebrow rose. Curious, John sat back down.

He watched the brunette dance—or try to dance, was more to the point—for the next fifteen minutes. She was a beautiful woman with dark hair and Elizabeth Taylor eyes. Her body was lush and provocative, curvy in all the right places. Big tits, round ass—gorgeous. But her dancing...

She didn't belong up there. That realization intrigued him all the more.

For the first five minutes John had wondered if all the falls and klutzy mistakes had been done on purpose, though he'd never heard of comedic stripping. It became rapidly apparent that, no, the horrific pole work was not an act and the brunette simply couldn't dance to save herself. When her fangs fell out and landed in a patron's expensive drink, well, that was the capper.

John's mouth curved into a smile. She definitely didn't belong up there.

He pulled out a crisp one hundred dollar bill and held it up so she'd see him and come closer. The blondes swarmed him like vultures, but he paid them no attention as he waited on the brunette to notice him. She never did. She was too busy biting her tongue in concentration as she danced—if one stretched the meaning of the word far enough—around the pole.

The two blondes prudently scurried over to different customers, aware that they wouldn't be getting that bill out of John's hand. His gaze was fixed on the clumsy brunette. When the object of his interest fell down and banged her knees for what had to be the fourth time, she managed to break one of her stilettos in the process. John grinned as he watched her take the shoes off and mutter something undecipherable under her breath. Barefoot, she continued to attack the pole, trying to climb up it for reasons unknown. It brought to mind an injured monkey attempting to get up a tree.

He chuckled. Comedic stripping had its values.

Wondering what she would do next, he was more than a little disappointed when the routine came to an abrupt end and the lights on stage faded to black. He decided to wait around for the next show, hoping she would be in it. If not, he'd find the owner and unsubtly ask for an introduction. He wasn't worried that minor formality would be denied — nobody ever told him no.

John inclined his head toward a waitress, indicating he wanted another bourbon. Shifting in his seat, it occurred to him that the brunette had kept him smiling, even laughing, for fifteen straight minutes.

She was the lousiest stripper he'd ever seen. She was awkward, accident-prone and danced like a rabid animal.

But she was also a miracle worker.

Chapter Four

Shelli was afraid she'd end up getting fired from the moment her fangs popped out. When the heel of her stiletto broke and she spent the rest of the routine dancing barefooted, well, she knew she was toast at that point. And she was right. Lynette handed her the proverbial walking papers within seconds of making it backstage. Shelli had realized there was no point in begging her ex-boss to let her keep the job. She sucked at stripping. Worse, an important client had been in the audience to witness all of tonight's mishaps. She might have cost Lynette some business deal or another.

John Calder. Shelli'd heard the name, of course, but had no idea which of the many men in the audience he had been. School kept her too busy to read tabloids or watch much television.

The male patrons all seemed to blend together in her mind anyway. They always had. The only man tonight who stood out from the others had been a really handsome blond guy seated toward the front. It wasn't his looks that had struck her, though. It was the quiet sadness in his eyes. She'd watched him from backstage before what had turned out to be her final show, but had no idea why she'd fixated on him in particular.

It had to be the eyes. They lent a certain vulnerability to an otherwise physically intimidating man.

Shelli frowned severely. She was probably being dramatically romantic. It wouldn't have been the first occasion. The last time she thought she'd seen vulnerability in a man's eyes it had turned out to be conjunctivitis.

Taking a deep breath, she pushed all contemplations of the brooding stranger out of her mind. Staring out the taxi's window, she turned her thoughts to finding a new part-time job. Try as she might, she couldn't think of any job but stripping that paid like a fulltime occupation while requiring half the hours.

There will be no more stripping!

Not that anyone in their right mind would hire her for it. Shelli rubbed her temples, feeling uncharacteristically dismal. Six months! That's all she needed. Her dream job awaited her once she earned her Ph.D.

The university was closing down after tomorrow's classes for a three-week holiday break. Thank goodness she had a mother to stay with because that meant the dorms were closing too, even the small facility that a few lucky graduate students got to keep residence in.

It also bought her time to find a new job. Somehow, Shelli decided, everything would work out, if for no other reason than it had to. In half a year she *would* be an anthropologist with a real career. She'd busted her ass for eight years and some change to make that dream a reality.

She wasn't good at stripping for people, but she was damn good at studying them.

* * * * *

He was becoming more than a little irritated.

John cursed under his breath as he listened to the dorm security guard tell Manuel that all the students had left campus for winter break, including the graduate students. He was beginning to wonder if his brunette—Shelli—would ever be found.

When she hadn't come out to perform another dance, John had immediately sought out the owner of *Venus Rising*. It had taken some doing, not to mention some cash, but he'd managed to finagle Shelli Rodgers' name and address out of the woman who had fired her.

"*Are you crazy?*" Lynette had sputtered out. "*You can't possibly want Shelli to work at Hotel Atlantis. She'd probably trip and puncture somebody's scrotum with her stilettos!*"

John half-snorted at the remembered warning. Lynette might have been right, but then, he had no interest in employing his brunette to fuck a man who wasn't him. He didn't even know what it was about her that drew his interest like a moth to a flame. She was pretty, yes, but he'd had pretty many times.

She made you smile. She forced you to enjoy being alive for fifteen straight minutes...

He wanted that feeling back. Even if it was only for another fifteen minutes.

"You okay, boss?"

John's head shot up. How could he be okay? He was irrationally obsessed with a woman he'd never so much as spoken to. If he ever found her, which was beginning to look like a very big if, she might turn out to be as boring and shallow as every other woman of his acquaintance.

He inclined his head toward Manuel. "I'm fine."

The driver frowned, obviously not believing him. "You might not be now, but you will be soon."

John's right eyebrow rose inquisitively.

"The security guard should be fired, but he told me exactly where to find Ms. Rodgers. Her mother lives about an hour's drive away and that's where she goes when the dorms close."

A dull pain flickered to life in John's chest. Any other man might have called it hope or pleasure. John was simply grateful to feel anything at all. "Excellent work," he murmured.

Manuel nodded. "Shall we go?"

"No. I'll go alone."

"You sure? I don't mind."

"You never mind, which I appreciate. But go home to Angelina. I'll take things from here."

Manuel's smile came slowly. "You got it that bad for the lady?"

"I don't even know the lady!" John snapped. He grunted, offended. "And yes."

Chapter Five

"I ain't eatin' this horse shit."

"Mama—"

"Don't 'Mama' me, Vanessa Ann Rodgers. I hate restaurant food, always have. I guess I could pick a booger out of my nose and eat that. Lord knows it'll taste better."

"Grandma!" Shelli half scolded and half laughed. She'd learned long ago there was no sense in getting embarrassed over her feisty grandmother's antics, but said grandmother was making the face of her daughter—Shelli's mom—heat up from all the unwanted attention their table was drawing. "Be nice! Mom's treating you to a dinner out so you don't have to cook."

"I like cookin', always have. I cooked for your granddad every night for forty-seven years before he up and died on me."

"I know, Mama," Vanessa said patiently, "but you can cook tomorrow night, can't you?"

"I'm with Grandma," Shelli's sister Lindsay announced. She stood up, eyeing the plate disdainfully. "This steak is garbage."

Shelli's nostrils flared. She wasn't in love with the food in this dive either, but there was no use in hurting their mom's feelings. She'd worked her ass off to pay for this outing. Lindsay worked her ass off for no one. "Beggars can't be choosers."

Lindsay rolled her eyes. "Whatever." She picked up her purse and hoisted it over one shoulder. "See you later, Miss Perfect."

"Where are you going?" their mother demanded.

"Out with friends."

"What time will you be home?"

"When I get there."

Furious, Shelli looked away from her sister before she said something they'd all regret. In the two days she'd been back home, all they seemed to do was fight. Sighing, she absently glanced around the diner. Luckily, the interest surrounding Grandma's rant had apparently waned. The other customers seemed wrapped up in their own conversations again.

A curious feeling stole over Shelli, a ripple of awareness that alerted her to the fact someone was watching her. She scanned the small diner again. Nothing.

"What's going on with Lindsay?" Shelli asked as she turned to watch her sister leave the diner. "Her behavior is terrible, Mom. Even for her."

Vanessa sighed. "I wish I knew. It's been this way since Daddy died."

"And getting worse," Shelli muttered.

"Give her time," Grandma cut in. "Everybody's got to deal with things in their own way and in their own time."

"I suppose you're right," Shelli said. "But I worry for her. She's not on drugs, is she?"

"No, no, nothing like that," Vanessa assured her.

"Positive?"

"Completely."

Shelli nodded. Her mom would know. She'd spent thirty-three years married to a drug addict, after all. Dad had tried to kick his addiction for years. In the end, the addiction had kicked him into an early grave.

Every time circumstances forced Shelli into remembering her dad's overdose, conflicting emotions were the inevitable result. Her brain, the logical part of her, recognized that her father had a horrible disease. But her heart, that damn organ mislabeled as being responsible for emotions, well, it had a mind of its own. Her heart believed that Dad should have loved his family more than getting high and feared that maybe he hadn't.

She sighed. Perhaps Lindsay's behavior wasn't surprising after all. She undoubtedly experienced the same contradictory emotions that, unbidden, still wreaked havoc on Shelli. Regardless, Lindsay was only two years younger than Shelli's twenty-nine. It was time to woman up and become a productive member of the family again.

Shelli blinked. That weird feeling was back. The sound of her mom and grandma bickering back and forth was drowned out by an acute awareness that someone was watching her. She scanned the diner another time.

Still nothing. Shelli frowned, wondering why that bizarre alertness persisted. Nobody was paying her any attention at all. Everyone was minding their own business and embroiled in their own conversations. She looked down to her plate.

"Horse shit," Grandma announced. She patted her overly bleached beehive into place. "Let's demand your money back, Vanessa Ann. I'll cook at home."

Shelli smiled at her grandmother's words as she glanced up. Her gaze clashed with a handsome blond man's. It was obvious he had overheard Grandma because he had an entertained look about him. She amusedly rolled her eyes at the stranger, giving him a *what-can-you-do-about-ornery-grandmas* look. He smiled back.

Shelli stilled. She squinted thoughtfully. There was something very familiar about that man, about those blue eyes...

Comprehension slowly dawned. Her eyes rounded.

Shelli's pulse soared as the golden-haired Adonis held her stare. He was that man from her last night working at the club. Oh no! What the hell was he doing here? She hysterically wondered if he'd approach their table and say something idiotic to her mother and grandmother, something that would alert them to the fact she'd been taking her clothes off for money.

The man rose from his seat.

Shit! Shit! Shit!

"Maybe we should go home and let Grandma cook," Shelli breathed out, returning her gaze to her family. "I'm suddenly not feeling very well."

"You see, Vanessa? The horse shit done poisoned my baby."

Vanessa frowned at her mother before turning to her daughter. "Sweetie, what's wrong? You look like you just saw a ghost."

"I think I'm just tired. My dissertation work has me drained."

"See there, Vanessa? Don't worry, Shel. If your mama insists we gotta stay here then Grandma will pick you a good booger to eat. It'll be healthier than this mess."

Shelli simultaneously groaned, gagged and laughed. The man was getting closer by the second. He had to stand in the vicinity of six and a half feet. Two more strides on those long legs and he'd be here. There was no escape.

"Mama, enough! Shelli, are you okay, honey? We can go home."

It was too late anyway. "No, no, I'll be fine. I know this meal cost you money you don't have."

"Never mind that. My budget can survive one meal."

"Yes, Shelli," a male voice broke in, drawing everyone's attention, "her budget will be fine because as it turns out, the meal is free."

"Free?" Grandma inquired.

"Yes," the man returned. "The diner is having a special today. Free food for all tables with cranky old ladies."

The Addiction

Grandma sniggered then picked up a French fry and popped it into her mouth. "Still tastes like horse shit, but it's free horse shit."

Shelli's attention, until then fully on the familiar stranger, was ripped in half. At that moment she realized why her grandmother always made a fuss when they went out to eat. Because she knew her daughter couldn't afford it and she wanted to spare her pride. The realization damn near made her cry.

"Sir," Vanessa began, "that's awfully nice of you, but I can't—"

"Please," the man softly interrupted. "I'd be honored to pay for the meal. Besides, you don't want your mother clearing out her nose for all the world to see, do you?" He winked. "Plus I'm a friend of your daughter's and I owed her one."

Shelli's world suddenly seemed very, very small and shrank further with every heartbeat. He owed her one? That had an ominous ring to it. What had she done to him?

Shit! Shit! Shit!

She searched her memories, trying to recall if she'd ever dumped hot coffee on his lap or accidentally whipped him in the eye during one of the bondage routines. Her sense of dread heightened. He wasn't the man whose scrotum she'd punctured with one of her stiletto heels, was he?

Oh God! Please don't be him! And if you are him, please tell me the surgeon was able to save your balls!

Stripping. What the hell had she been thinking?!

"Shelli! Why didn't you introduce us to your friend?" her mother chastised.

Shelli could barely form a coherent thought. Speaking was not an option.

"My name is John," the man offered, drawing the attention back to him. "John Calder."

Shelli's violet eyes widened. John Calder. The John Calder whom she had somehow managed to offend to the point of Lynette not getting to do business with him?

Holy shit. This could be worse than the scrotum incident.

* * * * *

"I just don't understand why you invited him to dinner," Shelli muttered to her mother. She continued peeling the potatoes as Grandma had instructed. "I was looking forward to a nice, quiet break at home with my family."

"It's one evening," Vanessa replied. "And he's your friend, isn't he?"

"Of course he is," Shelli said quickly. She wasn't about to contradict anything he'd told her family until she could get him alone and find out why he was here and what he was up to. "I'm just tired and grumpy. Sorry, Mom."

Vanessa smiled, but said nothing.

An hour later the doorbell rang. Yesterday's feeling of impending doom once again settled over Shelli. Her pulse quickened as she heard her mother welcome John Calder into their home.

Shelli took a deep breath and slowly exhaled. There was no sense in reacting to him like this. If he was here for revenge, making her sweat would only delight him. Plus there was always the small, extremely remote possibility that he had no intention of ratting her out to her family. But if he wasn't here to sing like a bird then why was he here? Only revenge made sense.

Maybe he was as attracted to me as I was to him...

Yeah, right. She rolled her eyes at her own musings. Men only did romantic shit like following women home in the movies. Serial killers might do it too, she allowed. Either way, not good.

The Addiction

"Shelli, bring the damn mashed potatoes out here, girl!" Grandma yelled from the house's small dining room. "This boy needs to eat!"

Shelli snorted as she picked up the mashed potatoes with one hand and a pitcher of gravy with the other. Grandma always thought everybody needed to eat, most especially when she was the chef.

She took another deep breath, counted to ten and slowly exhaled. She just hoped this dinner sped by so she could find out why John Calder had followed her from San Francisco, and what it was he wanted from her. Steeling herself, she held her head high and exited the kitchen.

She was even more beautiful tonight than she'd been yesterday at the diner, which was saying a lot. Last night she'd worn makeup and a cute little dress that clung to all her sexy curves. Here at her house, she was makeup free and clothed in loose-fitting white exercise pants that hung just below her navel. Her white t-shirt, which sported a black logo he didn't recognize, should have left everything to the imagination, but her large breasts kept that from happening, leaving her midriff exposed. Her long, dark, wavy hair was haphazardly piled on top of her head, giving her a disheveled, recently fucked appearance.

John shifted in his chair. He hoped like hell he wasn't asked to stand up for whatever reason because there would be no hiding his erection.

"What's with the suit?" Shelli's grandmother asked, drawing his attention. "We're simple folk 'round here. No need for all that."

"Mom," Vanessa said under her breath, though John could hear her. "Please be on your best behavior in front of Shel's friend."

"Well hells bells, Vanessa Ann," the feisty matriarch countered in her usual loud voice. "What did I say wrong now?"

"Good grief, Grandma," Lindsay said, frowning.

Vanessa emitted a long-suffering sigh. John glanced at Shelli, who stared back at him like a deer caught in headlights. He winked at her before turning his attention to her grandmother. "I had hoped to impress you with one of my best suits, Mrs. Rodgers. I suppose I'll have to think of another way to do that."

With the loud red lipstick, hopelessly out-of-style hairdo and horned glasses that bespoke of decades gone by, the older lady's grin could make anybody chuckle. Even a man who'd been dead inside for so long.

"I ain't Mrs. Rodgers, that old bitch died back before my Vanessa married her son. I'm Mrs. Vincent. But you can call me Arlene."

The eyebrows of all females at the dinner table rose in disbelief. Apparently their matriarch didn't permit most people to call her by her first name. A sense of pride and accomplishment swelled in John's chest. Ironic as it was, winning Arlene over made him feel better than closing any business deal ever had. He just hoped her granddaughter would prove to be as amenable.

"Thank you, Arlene. And thank you for this food. It's incredible."

Her smile widened. John smiled back. He hadn't lied or even stretched the truth, though. He'd eaten at damn near every five-star restaurant on the planet and none of them could hold a candle to this home-cooked meal. Creamy mashed potatoes smothered in gravy, country-fried steak, green beans and corn fritters...it was heaven.

"So how do you know my daughter?" Vanessa chimed in. A dead ringer for Shelli, she was a beautiful lady who'd aged

The Addiction

quite well. Her smile was as soft and unassuming as she appeared to be.

From his peripheral vision, John could see Shelli shifting in her chair. He had wondered why she hadn't gainsaid him back in the diner and now he understood. Her family didn't know that she had been supporting herself by stripping. The calculating businessman in him couldn't help but file that information away for later use, should the need to use it arise.

"We met at San Francisco State," John answered without missing a beat. "A good friend of mine owns the construction company that redesigned the Anthropology department's building."

Shelli cleared her throat. John didn't look away from her mother and grandmother, but could sense her apprehension. Clearly he had unnerved her. She now realized there was little about her he didn't know.

Good.

Vanessa nodded, satisfied with his answer, and the meal continued. The next hour seemed to fly by for John as they all traded stories, laughed and ate. The close-knit togetherness of this family was intriguing and fulfilling, even if it was as foreign to him as happiness. Shelli managed to let down her guard a time or two, laughing at some of Arlene's many stories and even a couple of his. Her dimples popped out when she laughed, making her impossibly more attractive.

Shelli wasn't the only one letting her guard down. John found himself not only giving truthful answers to the many questions asked of him, but expounding upon them and divulging memories of his own. He was careful to avoid certain topics, though. Specifically, his role as a glorified pimp.

All eyes were riveted on him as he told them amusing tales about everything from his last trip to the Congo to the time he was gored by a bull in Pamplona. The latter story was of particular interest to everyone, especially to the feisty old lady whose cackles grew on him more and more with each passing second.

"Right in the ass?" Arlene asked.

"Right in the ass," John confirmed.

She snickered and started to ask another question, but was interrupted by Shelli. He turned to look at her, knowing she would want to speak to him privately. He was surprised she had waited this long to make an excuse to get him alone. Her family didn't seem aware of her nervousness, but then neither did they realize she had a reason to be.

"Grandma, your pecan pie is probably done by now," Shelli said with what seemed a forced cheerfulness. "Would you excuse John and me for a moment before dessert?"

"Go on," Vanessa answered for her, smiling. "I'll get the coffee going while Grandma sees to the pie."

John stood up when Shelli did. "I can hardly wait for dessert," he told the table. "I've never tasted homemade pecan pie before."

Arlene clucked her tongue as though he'd admitted a cardinal sin. Thank God she was clueless about the pimp part. "Go on and take a walk with my Shel. We'll fix your problem when y'all get back."

John couldn't help but be amused. From the way Arlene spoke, one would think he had a venereal disease or multiple heads rather than a lack of experience eating homemade pecan pie.

"We'll be right back," Shelli announced before turning to walk toward the front door. "We won't be long."

Chapter Six

ಬಿ

Shelli didn't know what to think or how to feel. John Calder had been the perfect guest all through dinner. He hadn't said anything about *Venus Rising*, or even alluded to it. In fact, he'd been so pleasant and entertaining she'd almost found herself believing they were the friends he'd claimed them to be.

Except for the looks. She'd caught him staring at her more than once, his blue eyes raking over her face and breasts. She'd never felt so naked and aware of herself as she had in those moments. Not even up on a stage, where she'd worn nothing but a G-string and stiletto heels.

When they finally reached his car in the long gravel driveway, Shelli stopped and turned to look at John. He was so tall. And those muscles…not even an expensive Italian suit could hide them.

She took a deep breath and found the courage to meet his gaze. "What do you want from me?" she bluntly asked. There was no point in beating around the bush. "Why did you follow me here?"

His gaze bore into hers. He didn't answer for the longest time, so long in fact that she started to wonder if he ever would.

"I don't know," he murmured.

Shelli stilled. She wasn't certain how to respond. "You…you don't know?"

He shook his head, the movement almost imperceptible.

"Is it about Lynette? Are you angry that your business deal didn't go through? I'm sorry if I was the cause of that, but I assure you it wasn't—"

"Business deal?" John interrupted. He looked confused. "I don't know what you're talking about."

Their conversation grew stranger by the moment. "Lynette said something about a John Calder and my, uh, dancing, making her lose his business."

He snorted at that. His gaze, once distant, looked amused. "You're the worst stripper I've ever seen."

Shelli frowned. "I know!" she snapped. "But thank you for pointing that fact out."

"You made me laugh. I'd never seen a show quite so inept as yours."

Her cheeks reddened. She knew she was a lousy stripper, but hearing such a handsome man tell her he'd laughed at her performance still managed to sting her pride. Embarrassed and ashamed, she turned to walk away. A large, strong hand on her shoulder stopped her in her tracks.

"I didn't mean that in a bad way," John said quickly. "I can see how you'd take it like that, though."

Shelli's nostrils flared. She turned around and faced him once again. "You mean there's a *good* way to take that statement?"

That quiet sadness returned to his eyes, the same melancholia that had managed to attract and hold her attention as she'd watched him from backstage. This was the most bizarre conversation she's ever had. Logic dictated that the man was strange and she should run, yet her feet stayed firmly planted on the gravel driveway.

"I hadn't laughed in a long time," John said quietly. "It felt...well, it felt nice."

Silence.

Shelli's empathetic gaze raked over his face. "I'm sorry," she whispered.

He sighed and looked up to the stars. "I shouldn't have come here. I don't know why I did."

"It's okay," she assured him. "I'm glad I managed to make you laugh." Her smile was self-deprecating. "Even if it was for all the wrong reasons."

John agitatedly ran a hand over his jawline before meeting her gaze. "I have to go. I've imposed long enough and I need to get some sleep tonight before driving back to the city tomorrow."

Shelli would have insisted he stay for dessert, but his earlier show of vulnerability had obviously embarrassed him. "Are you sure?"

His smile was beautiful yet painfully sad. "I'm sure," he murmured. Holding her gaze, he reached for her left hand and drew it up to his lips. The chaste kiss was headier than it had the right to be. "Thank you," he said softly. "For everything."

And then he was gone. Shelli watched him get into his Jaguar and drive away. Her gaze followed his car long after it had disappeared into the country night.

* * * * *

John turned off the shower. He slowly worked the cheap motel towel down the length of him, his every movement feeling heavy and surreal. Stepping into a pair of cotton pajama pants, he made his way to the motel room's small bed and fell down onto it. Staring at the ceiling, he asked himself for the hundredth time why he had driven away from the only woman in the world who had been able to make him feel alive in God knows how long.

Because she's too good for me. Because she doesn't belong in my world any more than I want to stay in it. Because watching that beautiful, dimpled face become as hard and jaded as my own would be a disservice to the entire planet.

John sighed. He'd made a lot of mistakes in his life, and becoming a pimp was the worst of them. He wasn't the type to bring a woman down to his level. Especially not the woman responsible for waking up something inside him, something that made him smile, laugh and want to live.

Something that felt a lot like hope.

Shelli tossed and turned in her bed, trying to get comfortable. No matter what position she rolled into or how many damn sheep she tried to count, sleep continued to elude her. Falling onto her back, she gave up the fight and let herself think about him.

John Calder. That strange, handsome, fascinating man.

No man had ever made her feel heartbroken for him just by looking into his sad eyes. No man had ever made her stomach knot and race with butterflies from a mere kiss on the hand. She smiled. No man had ever been so gentlemanly as to kiss her hand before.

"I hadn't laughed in a long time. It felt...well it felt nice."

His words played over and over again in her mind like a beautiful, broken record. To think that her clumsy pole dancing, of all things, was the impetus to his laughter, to following her back home for reasons even he didn't understand...

He might be toying with you, Shel. A man as powerful as him would know all the right moves in any game he chooses to play.

She bit her lip. Deep inside, she didn't believe that. Human behavior was her specialty and all her senses screamed that this man, this familiar stranger, was as broken and empty as his eyes promised he was. She could smell desperation from ten paces. Lord knows her father had reeked of it.

"I couldn't save Dad," Shelli whispered to the walls. "I sure as hell can't save John Calder."

Maybe he didn't need saving. Perhaps all John needed was a friend, someone to be there for him while he found the energy to surmount whatever mental hurdle had sent him chasing after a woman he didn't even know.

John had said he would be driving back to the city in the morning, which meant he was still here tonight. There was only a single motel anywhere in the area so she knew exactly where he had to be staying. Once he was gone, she might never get the chance to see him again. San Francisco was a huge metropolis, nothing at all like her Podunk hometown.

Shelli ran her fingers through her hair. What she was contemplating doing was sheer lunacy. He was a stranger whom she'd known for all of two days and she had spent a grand total of two hours with him.

"Thank you. For everything."

She was insane. He was insane. The entire situation was insane…

Shelli bolted upright and scurried out of bed to get dressed. Her mind was made up. Fumbling for the keys to her car, she quietly left the house so as not to wake anyone.

"I'm an idiot," she muttered to herself as she slid the key into the ignition. "John Calder, you better not be a serial killer."

At least she was certain he didn't have conjunctivitis. There was nothing pink about those haunting blue eyes.

Chapter Seven

There was nothing on television and John couldn't sleep. The insomnia refused to give him some peace, even when all his mental defenses were down. He hated being awake like this at night. It gave him too much time to think, too much time to ponder ideas that were selfish to even consider.

It would be so easy to end this. One well-placed bullet and no more pain. Who would I be hurting but myself?

Jack and his sister Sheri was who. Maybe even Manuel.

John sighed. He picked up the remote and switched off the television set. He was starting to feel like a vampire in a really dark movie. Too dead to feel alive, but unwilling to meet the dawn.

A knock on the motel room door startled him from his thoughts. Nobody knew where he was, so John couldn't imagine whom it could be. He stood up and made his way to the door. If he was lucky it would be an armed robber who ended it all for him. The pain would be gone and he'd have had no hand in causing it.

"Yeah," he said, his voice monotone as he opened the door. "What do you—"

John stilled, completely caught off guard. But then, she was good at doing that to him. "Shelli?"

Shelli's heart pounded in her chest as she stared up at the very tall, half-naked man standing before her. It took a millisecond to ascertain that she had been correct about his musculature. Sweet lord above, he was beautiful. John Calder looked like he'd been chiseled from stone by Michelangelo himself.

He had the richly tanned skin of a man who spent a lot of time in the water. His chest was smooth, his nipples the sexiest she'd ever seen on a male. Her gaze lowered to where a line of dark-gold hair began just below his navel and trailed down into his pajama pants. His erection was long and thick, protruding against the fabric.

Her breath hitched. Her gaze flew up to meet his.

Neither of them spoke. Neither of them moved. Time seemed to stand still. His eyes were tinged with sadness, yet she could sense an even stronger emotion inside them fighting to win.

Her heart wrenched. He made her feel like he was a dying man and she was the only person on earth who could save him.

Shelli closed the door behind her, her gaze still locked with John's. Without a word, she began to undress. She lifted her shirt up and over her head, allowing her breasts to spring free. His eyes grew heavy-lidded, his breathing ragged, as he memorized her breasts with his gaze. Shelli tossed the forgotten garment to the floor as a knot of desire coiled in her belly and tightened her nipples.

She pushed down her exercise pants and G-string simultaneously, bending over slightly to discard them. Shelli kicked off her sandals then stood fully upright, her stare once again locking with his. John's gaze rose to her hair before lowering back down to meet her wide eyes. Understanding what he wanted, she raised her hands to the clip holding her loose bun in place and let it fall to the ground. Her long, dark hair pooled around her, cascading in wavy ringlets.

Her breathing grew heavier, causing her breasts to rise and fall. His eyes, once dead, seared with life. Shelli needed him to touch her like she needed air to breathe. She'd never desired any man like she did John.

She hoped she hadn't misread the situation and that he wanted her just as badly. The thought weakened her, leaving her to feel rawer and more exposed than she had ever felt before.

John stared down at Shelli, her stature so tiny compared to his. He was accustomed to tall models and actresses, but found himself preferring this height differential. Shelli might have been short, but there was nothing weak or vulnerable about her. Those attributes lay within him, he knew.

It scared John how much he needed this woman, a person who was all but a stranger to him. The feeling frightened him so powerfully that he found himself contemplating whether or not he should touch her. It would take only a single caress, he realized, and then he would be touching her all night long.

And then what about tomorrow? Touch her again? Bring this wonderful, generous woman down to his level? Make her life as wretched as his own had become?

John took a deep breath, hoping to regain control over the situation. But when he looked down and saw the fear of rejection dimming round, violet eyes that had always shone bright, it was his undoing. There was nothing inadequate about her, only about himself.

"John?" Shelli whispered. Her voice quivered almost imperceptibly.

She wanted him as much as he needed her. There was no fight left in him.

John reached out for her and Shelli flew into his arms. He picked her up and kissed her with all the hunger inside him, groaning when she wrapped her legs around his waist. He carried her to the bed as their tongues clashed and dueled, his mouth ravenously covering hers.

Falling with her onto the bed, John settled between her thighs as their kiss deepened and intensified. Shelli moaned and reached for his pajama bottoms, her hands working them down as far as they could manage before settling on his ass and squeezing. John groaned into her mouth, then broke their kiss long enough to get completely naked. He threw aside the unwanted clothing and settled back between her legs.

"John," Shelli panted, her face flushed, "John— I— Please."

She sounded as aroused and confused as he was. Like she wanted everything and more, but wasn't certain what *more* entailed.

His breathing heavy, John palmed Shelli's large breasts. The sound of her gasp made his balls tighten and his cock grow impossibly harder. Lowering his head, he pushed her tits together, giving his mouth access to both. She whimpered as his tongue curled around one of her stiff nipples and drew it into his mouth, then moaned as he began to suck it.

"Oh my God," Shelli breathed out, her voice coming in gasps, "Oh John— *Oh my God.*"

He growled around her nipple, having never felt so possessive of a woman in his life. He took his time, sucking on it from root to tip, her sounds of pleasure heightening his arousal. John released her nipple with a popping sound and covered the other one with his mouth. He sucked it hard, and harder still, her every moan forcing him closer to the edge.

He didn't want to come on her. He wanted to come *in* her.

His breathing heavy, John tore his mouth away from her nipple, a second heady popping sound underlining that fact. "You're so fucking sexy," he said thickly, grabbing his cock by the base. He settled himself between her legs as he guided his shaft to her wet opening. "I want you so damn bad, Shelli."

John stared into her wide eyes, waiting for her to say she wanted him just as much. Shelli didn't speak, but reared her hips at him instead, telling him without words everything he needed to know. He couldn't wait another second to be inside her. His jaw tight, John groaned as he surged deep inside her tight pussy.

Shelli's loud and immediate scream of pain startled him, forcing him to still within her. "Shel?" he murmured, his gaze once again locking with hers.

"I'm okay," she whispered, smiling up at him. "Just give me a second to adjust or something."

"But what's the mat—"

He blinked. His eyes rounded as comprehension slowly dawned.

Shelli blushed and looked away. John grabbed her chin and gently forced it back so she would see him.

"Yes," she said, her voice tinted with embarrassment, "I'm a virgin. Or I mean I *was* a virgin."

A virgin. A stripping virgin. Holy shit.

He wanted to say that she shouldn't feel ashamed, then show her he meant it by making slow, sweet love to her. He wanted to do and say a lot of things, but the primitive, territorial part of his brain could focus on one thing and one thing only…

No man had ever fucked her.

John began to move within her, trying to be gentle while realizing he was being anything but. Shelli accepted him anyway, her hands massaging his ass while he rutted inside her like an animal. "My pussy," John gritted out, his thrusts going deeper. "All mine."

"*John.*"

He rode her harder than he should have, her tight, sticky cunt sucking his cock back in on every outstroke. He'd fucked hundreds of women before, but none of them had made him feel as alive and important as he felt in this moment. None of them had made him feel anything at all.

He fucked Shelli harder, glutting himself on her cunt. The sound of wet flesh slapping against wet flesh filled the tiny motel room, heightening his arousal. His jaw tightened as he fucked her deeper and faster, over and over, again and again and again.

"I'm coming," John rasped out, his voice possessive and gravelly. He held onto Shelli tightly, his cock branding her pussy as his with each stroke. "*Here I come, baby.*"

She bit his neck and squeezed his ass, sending him over the edge. John growled out his orgasm, his hips rapidly pistoning back and forth as his entire body shuddered and convulsed on top of hers. "Shelli—Jesus—*Shelli.*"

Shelli held him as he rode out the waves of pleasure, pulling him closer as he spurted his hot cum inside her. She whispered words he couldn't make sense of, but which comforted him nonetheless. Her arms wrapped tightly around him as he collapsed on top of her. They stayed that way for a long moment, neither of them speaking.

Finally, John slowly rolled off her, their embrace never breaking as he pulled Shelli to his chest. He needed to make love to her right, show her that he could do much better than rutting in her sweet pussy like an animal. Maybe then she'd never want to leave him.

It was his last coherent thought before succumbing to sleep.

* * * * *

Shelli awoke to the feel of her clit being gently lapped at. Her eyes flew open on a gasp. "John," she murmured, threading her fingers through his hair. "That feels so good."

Apparently *good* wasn't enough praise. His tongue curled around her sensitive clit and drew it into the heat of his mouth. She moaned, her hips instinctively rearing up. John pressed his face in closer, harder, and sucked on the aroused piece of flesh. Shelli groaned, the coiling knot of desire in her belly unlike anything she'd ever felt before. She'd experienced pleasure from masturbating, but no amount of self-stimulation could have prepared her for this moment.

John moaned around her clit, his lips and tongue working her into a frenetic state. She wrapped her legs around his neck, wanting his face pressed as tightly against her pussy as humanly possible. Her nipples stiffened as she hazily watched him suck on her.

"*Mmmm*," John purred, sucking her clit in a steady rhythm, "*mmmmm.*"

The coil sprang loose. Shelli burst on a loud groan.

"*Oh my God!*" Shelli cried out. Her hips thrashed and her nipples jutted up impossibly farther. "*John!*"

He licked her, lapped at her, drank of her. Blood rushed to her face, heating it, then to her nipples and clit, making them beyond sensitive.

And still he didn't stop. He sucked on her aroused flesh again, forcing her body to a new, unchartered height where pain and pleasure mingled to become one. The next orgasm assaulted Shelli so hard she could barely remember her own name.

"*Oh John! Oh. My. Gohhhhhhhd!*"

Shelli screamed out her orgasm, her entire body convulsing. She came violently, with a ferociousness she'd not known was possible. John praised her in moans as he lapped up her juices, his breathing growing heavy and his hands rubbing her thighs.

"I need you," she gasped, pulling at him, wanting him inside her. "Please."

John kissed his way up her body, from her navel to her lips, leaving nothing to neglect. He hovered over Shelli for a suspended moment, those haunting blue eyes piercing her soul. "Not like I need you," he murmured. Her eyes widened. He thrust inside her.

Shelli moaned, accepting him. She prepared herself for the same hard ride he'd given her their first time together, but John surprised her again. He plunged in and out of her slowly and steadily, letting her body adjust and learn. His cock was steel-hard, but his movements were controlled and gentle.

Shelli smiled into John's gaze as he made love to her.

*****

They spent three more glorious days and nights together, never apart, both of them laughing, happy and complete. When they weren't joking around or making love, they had serious conversations about their lives, both of them being honest with the other about everything from their worst fears, to their jobs and schooling, even touching on sensitive subjects like religion and politics.

Yet despite their definite bond, regardless of the fact that his beautiful, haunted gaze had grown warm and alive, Shelli also knew John was guarding a part of himself. Whenever the moment grew too serious or too poignant, his blue eyes would lock up, as if searching for that dead space that was at once lonely and familiar to him.

She loved him. It was crazy—some would say impossible—to truly love someone after only a few short days, but Shelli was certain of her feelings. Female intuition whispered to her not to say the words, not to put her heart out there to get ripped to pieces, but in the end she decided that if he left her, that damn organ would get smashed to bits whether she'd been honest or not.

"I love you, John," Shelli said softly, accepting him inside her again. He stilled for a moment, but said nothing. "It's okay," she promised, stroking his back. "Just know that I do."

"Shelli…I—"

"Shhh." Her smile was genuine, making her dimples pop out. "I love you."

John groaned as he buried himself in her pussy. He made love to her as if his life depended on it, as if he was a dying man performing his final act on earth. On the fourth morning, Shelli knew why.

She awoke to an empty room, just as she'd feared she would one morning soon. The motel room was clean and everything that belonged to him was gone, as if she'd dreamt John's very presence there. Steeling herself against a wave of unwanted emotion and fighting back tears that threatened to spill, her gaze floated to the room's sole table, and to the note lying on it. She stood up and walked over to it, her heart heavy.

Dear Shelli,

I want to thank you for the best four days of my life. I realize this note is a cowardly way to end things, but I couldn't have held strong if we'd talked instead. Please trust me that this decision is for the best because you deserve a much better man than I'll ever be. I love you too, sweetheart, and I always will. That's why I have to let you go.

Forever, John

Shelli read the note at least a dozen times before lowering her gaze and clutching the piece of paper to her heart. Unable to stave off the inevitable a moment longer, she cried softly as hot tears streamed down her cheeks.

Chapter Eight
One Year Later

ಸಿ

John Calder sat in the back of his limousine, his blue gaze watching the familiar scenery whiz by. It had been almost a year to the day since he'd last seen or spoken to Shelli, but in his mind it might as well have been yesterday. Not a day had gone by over the past twelve months that he hadn't thought about her, hadn't missed her. It had taken him far too long to get his shit together and evolve into a man worthy of her, but the former had come to pass even if the latter had not.

I know you must hate me, Shel. I just hope you can figure out a way to forgive me.

He glanced at his watch. Twenty more minutes and he'd reach her family's home.

Taking a deep breath and exhaling slowly, John wondered if Shelli even knew he was on his way. He'd spoken to her grandmother, Arlene, not to her.

Feeling increasingly nervous, John passed the remainder of the ride rehearsing every possible argument Shelli might throw his way to try to get him to go back from where he'd come. He couldn't do that, though — not again. He might have to spend the next ten years of his life getting her to understand that fact, but he was ready and willing to do whatever it took to get her back.

I need you, Shelli. I don't deserve you, but I need you...

John had gone through a lot to prepare himself for this moment in time. He'd wrestled with every mental demon a man can have and knew he was a better person for it. *Hotel Atlantis,* once the world's most expensive brothel, was now a relic of the past. He'd had the compound demolished and had taken great pleasure in watching as it smoldered down to cinders, smoke and ash. His best buddy Jack, the contractor he'd hired to do the deed, had been there beside him as he'd watched it go down. Jack understood the symbolism behind the act without either of them having to speak it aloud.

No more pimping. No more wondering how many marriages he'd ruined with that place. No more worrying that one of his former employees might have gotten emotionally scarred during her time as a prostitute.

No more overlooking every principle he'd once held dear in the name of a dollar.

Finally, John was at peace. The only part of the puzzle missing now was Shelli. He could only pray that somehow, some way, someday, she would forgive him.

* * * * *

"Girl, what did I say? I done told you not to contact the man! He needs to realize things on his own."

"She didn't, Grandma!" Lindsay sputtered in way of defense. "If you had listened while she spoke instead of thinking up your rebuttal, you'd know that."

"Oh horse pucky."

Shelli grinned at her sister from across the dinner table. Lindsay had done a lot of growing up in the past year and Shelli couldn't have been prouder. It was as if something inside Lindsay had finally snapped and awakened.

"It's true," Shelli's mom confirmed. "John has been contacting Shelli's boss, not Shelli."

"Dr. Torrence?" Grandma asked.

"Yes," Vanessa answered. "As it turns out, John's best friend Jack is married to Kris Torrence."

"*Jack*? Well I'll be damned."

"Yep," Shelli confirmed. "They're still newlyweds, actually. They got married about three months after I earned my Ph.D., right after I had Johnny."

Johnny. Shelli smiled from the mere thought of her son. Her unexpected pregnancy had shocked the entire family but it had also brought them closer together. She suspected that a huge part of Lindsay's transformation had come as a result of Shelli's beloved baby boy. Lindsay was turning out to be the world's greatest aunt and Johnny the planet's most spoiled nephew. Shelli wouldn't have had it any other way.

"So she's been married to Jack almost three months?" Grandma asked.

"Roughly," Shelli confirmed.

"I remember the stories you used to tell about the fights them two would have." Grandma shook her head. "How the hell did they go from that to saying their 'I-Dos'?"

Shelli shrugged, not in the mood to go into detail. Needless to say, the news of their marriage had thrown her for a loop too. But that was a different story altogether.

At any rate, her boss kept insisting that Shelli tell her who Johnny's father was. They were more than employer and employee, Krissy had harped, they were also friends. Shelli had known that to be true so had confided in her as soon as she felt ready to tell the full story to someone outside her immediate family.

Shelli hadn't gotten quite the *"oh-my-God-I've-read-about-that-asshole-in-the-papers"* reaction that she'd expected. Instead, Krissy had been concerned for her *and* for John—she felt he should know about the baby he'd fathered. When Shelli admitted she didn't know how to contact him, so had named her son for him instead, Krissy had become giddy, bubbly and excited.

She knew John, as it turned out. She knew him quite well.

Stranger still was the doctor's insistence that things would work out, and John would see the error of his ways and come crawling back. The latter part had failed to happen, but at least John now knew of his son and wanted to see him. He had phoned this morning and asked Grandma if he could come out to the family house to talk to Shelli, so it seemed obvious Krissy had spilled the paternal beans. Grandma had told John, "it's about damn time," which was her surly way of saying yes.

A selfish part of Shelli wished that Krissy had been right and John was coming back into her life because he missed and needed her. But the biggest piece of her, the part called Mommy, was just glad her son had a father who wanted him. At least she hoped that was the case…

Shelli worried her lip. The troublesome thought that John might be coming to the house only to tell her he wanted nothing to do with their son permeated her consciousness for the first time. Her nostrils flared as feelings of anger and maternal protectiveness swept over her. Johnny was the center of her universe. If his father didn't feel the same way then he wasn't good enough to be in their lives anyway.

The doorbell rang, causing Shelli's heart rate to skyrocket. All eyes flew to her. She took a deep breath and slowly exhaled.

"Go on, girl," Grandma said, nodding her head. "He's either a man who done learnt a good lesson or a fool who needs to be sent away. Go see which it is. And be back here in time for my pecan pie."

Shelli pasted on a serene face and stood up. "You only make them at Christmastime, so I wouldn't miss a bite for the world."

Her hands felt clammy. She rubbed them together then smoothed out her jeans. Taking one last deep breath, Shelli made her way to the front door and opened it, but saw no one standing there. Frowning, she slipped outside, closing the door behind her.

Sensing someone's gaze boring into her, Shelli slowly turned her head. John stood next to the nativity scene in the front yard. He was dressed to the nines as always, in what had to be an endless supply of designer suits. She should have felt frumpy in comparison wearing only jeans and a sweatshirt, but she didn't.

Somewhere between closing the door and making eye contact with him, her heartbeat had picked up again. Perhaps it was the smoldering way John was looking at her, studying her. Perhaps it was simply because she was in his presence again at long last. She bowed her head, feeling nervous as he approached.

"I love you, Shelli."

Her head shot up and her eyes widened. She hadn't expected that.

Their gazes clashed and held. She stared into his eyes, those beautiful, soulless eyes that always flickered with life in her presence. Her heart wrenched at his words, but she didn't know how she should feel or if he could be believed.

"I don't expect you to forgive me any time soon," John continued, his voice sounding raw with emotion, "but I can't let you go again. I don't care who you're dating or even if you're married. I can't live without you."

The look on his face was determined, his jaw set. She opened her mouth to speak, but nothing came out.

"God, I've missed you," he said hoarsely. "You are even more beautiful than I remembered in my fantasies, which is saying a lot."

"John," Shelli began, "please—"

"No!" he barked. "I'm begging you to tell me it's not too late! I'll never walk away again, Shel. *Never.*"

"John," Shelli said with quiet conviction, "I would never keep you from seeing him. You don't have to pretend to have feelings you don't in order to be in his life."

John blinked. "*His* life?" A possessive glare stole over his features. "Who," he asked icily, "is *he*?"

The wailing sound of a hungry three-month-old punctured the ensuing silence. John watched, his stoic expression unreadable, as Shelli's mom opened the door and handed their son to her. "I think he's ready for dinner," Vanessa whispered. She smiled at John before slipping back inside.

John didn't speak for a long moment. His gaze flicked back and forth between mother and son. Shelli grinned down at Johnny, his dark-gold hair standing straight up as though he'd been playing with a light socket. Once he was smiling, she looked back up at his father.

"You had a baby," John murmured, his eyes unblinking.

Shelli's nose wrinkled. He wasn't making any sense. "Well yeah."

They stood there in silence for a long minute. Finally John said, his voice filled with conviction, "I don't care. I'll raise him as my own."

What the hell are you talking about? "Raise him as your own?" Shelli repeated. *Have you gone insane?!* "I would hope so," she smiled, "since he *is* your own."

All color seemed to drain from John's face. Shelli's smile faltered and her eyes widened as the truth hit them both at the same time. John Calder was a father and hadn't even known as much until this very moment. She took a cue from him, fairly certain her own color was draining at a rapid rate.

"Kris didn't tell you?"

"No," he rasped.

"Oh my God."

"You took the words right out of my mouth."

They stood there for what felt an eternity, staring at each other and their baby. Shelli's heart began beating out another wild tune. He had come back for her—*for her*! And if the look in John's eyes was any indication, he was happier than she'd ever thought he could be with the knowledge that she was now a package deal.

"Can I hold him?" John asked quietly, his eyes misty.

"Don't cry or I will too!" Shelli promised in a shaky voice. She hoped her smile radiated the warmth and joy she felt. "And of course you can."

He slowly held out his hands. "John," Shelli said, handing him their baby, "meet Johnny."

A single tear rolled down John's cheek as father and son stared at each other, mesmerized. Or at least father did. Son was too busy trying to make a meal out of his dad's tie to get awestruck by anything else. John chuckled, forcing Shelli to grin.

John's gaze flew back to Shelli. "Can I hold you too?"

A sensible woman would have made him grovel for at least another month. Her pride might even have caused her to refuse him altogether, whether still in love with him or not. But Shelli was the world's worst now-former stripper. Sensible wasn't in her vocabulary. Thank God!

"Why, John Calder," Shelli whispered, smiling, "I thought you'd never ask."

Also by Jaid Black

eBooks:

Trek Mi Q'an Series
- The Empress' New Clothes
- Seized
- No Mercy
- Enslaved
- No Escape
- No Fear
- Dementia
- Devilish Dot
- Never a Slave
- Guide to Trek Mi Q'an

Single Titles
- Adam & Evil
- After the Storm *(writing as Tia Isabella)*
- Before the Fire *(writing as Tia Isabella)*
- Bossy & Clyde
- Breeding Ground
- Death Row: The Trilogy
- Death Row: Besieged
- God of Fire
- Politically Incorrect: Stalked
- Politically Incorrect: Subjugated
- Sins of the Father
- The Hunger
- The Mastering
- The Obsession
- The Possession

- Tremors
- Vanished
- Warlord

Multiple Author Anthologies
- "The Beckoned" in *Ellora's Cavemen: Tales from the Temple IV*
- "Seeds of Yesterday" in *Ellora's Cavemen: Legendary Tails IV*
- "The Addiction" in *Something Wicked This Way Comes: Volume 1*
- "Fatman & Robyn" in *Something Wicked This Way Comes: Volume 2*

Print Books:

After the Storm *(writing as Tia Isabella)*

Breeding Ground

Death Row: The Trilogy

Ellora's Cavemen: Legendary Tails IV *(anthology)*

Ellora's Cavemen: Tales from the Temple IV *(anthology)*

Enchained *(anthology)*

Manaconda *(anthology)*

Notorious

Something Wicked This Way Comes: Volume 1 *(anthology)*

Something Wicked This Way Comes: Volume 2 *(anthology)*

The Best of Jaid Black

The Possession

Trek Mi Q'an: Conquest

Trek Mi Q'an: Enslaved

Trek Mi Q'an: Lost in Trek

Trek Mi Q'an: No Mercy

Trek Mi Q'an: Seized

Trek Mi Q'an: The Empress' New Clothes
Wedded Bliss *(anthology)*

10th Anniversary Additions

Death Row: The Trilogy

Notorious *(Sins of the Father, The Hunger, Politically Incorrect: Stalked)*

The Best of Jaid Black *(Tremors, The Obsession, Vanished)*

The Possession

About Jaid Black
ಐ

Jaid Black is the pseudonym for Ellora's Cave's owner and founder Tina M. Engler. She has been featured in every available news outlet, from the Washington Post and L.A. Times to Forbes magazine, Fox News and the Montel Show. Ms. Engler was officially recognized by Romantic Times Magazine with their first ever Trail Blazer award as the mastermind of erotic romance as you know and love it today. Writing as Jaid Black, her books have received numerous distinctions, including a nomination for the Henry Miller award for the best literary sex scene written in the English language.

ಐ

The author welcomes comments from readers. You can find her website and email address on her author bio page at www.ellorascave.com.

Tell Us What You Think

We appreciate hearing reader opinions about our books. You can email us at Service@ellorascave.com (when contacting Customer Service, be sure to state the book title and author).

Why an electronic book?

We live in the Information Age—an exciting time in the history of human civilization, in which technology rules supreme and continues to progress in leaps and bounds every minute of every day. For a multitude of reasons, more and more avid literary fans are opting to purchase e-books instead of paper books. The question from those not yet initiated into the world of electronic reading is simply: *Why?*

1. ***Price.*** An electronic title at Ellora's Cave Publishing runs anywhere from 40% to 75% less than the cover price of the exact same title in paperback format. Why? Basic mathematics and cost. It is less expensive to publish an e-book (no paper and printing, no warehousing and shipping) than it is to publish a paperback, so the savings are passed along to the consumer.

2. ***Space.*** Running out of room in your house for your books? That is one worry you will never have with electronic books. For a low one-time cost, you can purchase a handheld device specifically designed for e-reading. Many e-readers have large, convenient screens for viewing. Better yet, hundreds of titles can be stored within your new library—on a single microchip. There are a variety of e-readers from different manufacturers. You can also read e-books on your PC or laptop computer. (Please note that Ellora's Cave does not endorse any specific brands.

You can check our website at www.ellorascave.com for information we make available to new consumers.)

3. *Mobility.* Because your new e-library consists of only a microchip within a small, easily transportable e-reader, your entire cache of books can be taken with you wherever you go.
4. *Personal Viewing Preferences.* Are the words you are currently reading too small? Too large? Too... ANNOYING? Paperback books cannot be modified according to personal preferences, but e-books can.
5. *Instant Gratification.* Is it the middle of the night and all the bookstores near you are closed? Are you tired of waiting days, sometimes weeks, for bookstores to ship the novels you bought? Ellora's Cave Publishing sells instantaneous downloads twenty-four hours a day, seven days a week, every day of the year. Our webstore is never closed. Our e-book delivery system is 100% automated, meaning your order is filled as soon as you pay for it.

Those are a few of the top reasons why electronic books are replacing paperbacks for many avid readers.

As always, Ellora's Cave welcomes your questions and comments. We invite you to email us at Service@ellorascave.com or write to us directly at Ellora's Cave Publishing Inc., 1056 Home Avenue, Akron, OH 44310-3502.

Make each day more *EXCITING* With our

Ellora's Cavemen Calendar

www.EllorasCave.com

Ellora's Cave Romanticon

Annual convention
for women who
refuse to behave

www.ECRomanticon.com
For additional info contact: conventions@ellorascave.com

Discover for yourself why readers can't get enough of the multiple award-winning publisher Ellora's Cave. Be sure to visit EC on the web at www.ellorascave.com to find erotic reading experiences that will leave you breathless. You can also find our books at all the major e-tailers (Barnes & Noble, Amazon Kindle, Sony, Kobo, Google, Apple iBookstore, All Romance eBooks, and others).

www.ellorascave.com